GW01086913

To Mary –
Antony …

The Dorset Arms

A GHOSTLY STORY

all the best

Bonx Trigwell

Bonx Trigwell

Pen Press

First published in Great Britain by Pen Press

All paper used in the printing of this book has been made from wood grown in managed, sustainable forests.

ISBN13: 978-1-907499-82-1

Printed and bound in the UK
Pen Press is an imprint of Indepenpress Publishing Limited
25 Eastern Place
Brighton
BN2 1GJ

A catalogue record of this book is available from
the British Library

Cover design by Jacqueline Abromeit

An introduction by Aimee Quigley

Dear B,

First of all, let me thank you for allowing me to read your book. I think it's a great honor to read a persons writing. So, thank you.

I like the character Digger. There are a lot of thoughtful descriptions about nature around his part of the story (as well as with Anne Tree's). Those descriptions are beautiful. I like his humble way. And his story is a good one to start with as it introduces you to the beginnings of East Grinstead.I like that he died so suddenly. The tension was excellent on page 23 - the supposed fire in the basement. You write well for suspense. Wilf's ghost is straight out of a horror movie. It Freaks me out just to think of it. Mary's story is wickedly sad and beautifully written. Brian's such an Ass-hole. Andrew and Elizabeth's story is cool. It's Very easy to identify with them. At least it is for me - because it's modern day and their younger. But, I enjoyed that story and I think there are more stories along that vein. Of relationships and what else Andrew does - (could it be a memoir?). I like that there is real love and real loss there. The dialogue is good with them too. Smarmy Jackson is so smarmy-"Another delightful creation from the superlative fromagerie..." - Good dialog there. I really enjoyed the chaos and fun in 1991 - with the 101. The characters and the energy were totally rock and roll and crazy. I do think that it could be its own story also. Clearly - this is a memoir? Captain Lancaster- that was short and sad. You get the feeling that his life passed him by. His story was more about what he didn't have a chance to do that what he did do. His ghost is excellent with the jingling and the eyes in the painting. _ Quite ghostly. Eddy was well described. Think you have a good talent in describing what its like at war and what its like for the veterans when they return. You describe his memories well and convey the horror. The story that follows - with the basement room with newspapers- is chilling. I can imagine being there and finding that room. It felt so creepy and interesting. I wanted to go there and discover it myself

I like that the ghosts are all hanging out at the end. They are peaceful and I like that. I see the irony - the world that punished them is now being punished while they are happy and peaceful.

I didn't always follow the connection between the times at the end of the stories and what they meant. I'm sure if I looked back it would make sense but it wasn't obvious right away. Now - Dear young Bonx, Clearly, you have a penchant for the erotic. Occasionally I felt like I was reading an erotic novel. That is great, but, I'm just not sure where it fits in with ghost stories and the Dorset. I'm not sure if I Could suggest that you not be so graphic. Because, a writer has to enjoy what they are writing about. Maybe, you should write a purely erotic novel as well. It would be good. Have you read any? They're like stories with bits of sex. Actually their like sex with a bit of story. I don't want to steer you away from your detailed descriptions necessarily - because you describe stuff well - but - who's meant to be reading it? If you want it to be sellable you might need to tone it down to emphasize the stories more than the details of the stories.

Sometimes I felt like I was reading this sensitive, descriptive story about a person - and enjoying that - and then they were naked and swinging their nuts around. It was just a bit shocking and I wasn't sure where it was going. If I picked out the book from an erotic section of a book store - then I would expect it and hope that it would continue. But, this looks like a book you'd get in a fiction or history section, or a local section and I think that you'd expect this book to be about the ghost stories primarily. You may have some old ladies a little upset about your details. So maybe make two different books. And all those comments are only said because I'm thinking of sellibility - lots of readers. If this book remains a book for friends then it's perfect: the way it is because it's so totally you - a big blend of everything - and that's awesome. Oh - a couple other things...I really liked the way you tied in the old stories and then the ghost stories that related to them. That was well crafted. Plus, you definitely have a great talent for description and scenery. I could SEE the pub and the people- I could smell it. AND - your dialog between characters is GREAT. That's so hard to do. All and all it was a fun read - I totally enjoyed it and I think you have a true talent. It made me really want to see the Dorset again.

Please keep writing!

Aimee Quigley May 2009.

P.S. I know this was wickedly long but it feels right to give a lot of feedback to a friend who put a lot into something

The Dorset Arms

East Grinstead

FRESCO.-CROMWELL HOUSE, E: GRINSTEAD.1598

East Grinstead began as a Saxon village. Its name means green place. By the time of the Domesday Book (1086) it was quite a large village. In the 13th century East Grinstead became a town. In 1247 East Grinstead was given a charter (a document granting the people certain rights). The charter confirmed the right to hold weekly markets. It also granted East Grinstead an annual fair. In the Middle Ages fairs were like markets but they were held only once a year and they attracted buyers and sellers from a wide area. From 1516 East Grinstead had two fairs.

The first Title the Earl of Dorset was created in 1411. Sir Thomas Sackville (Lord Buckhurst) (1536-1608) was a favourite of Queen Elizabeth 1st, his second cousin; He was made Lord High Treasurer in 1599 and the title the Earl of Dorset was created in 1604.

In the eighteenth century the Dorset was almost rebuilt, using some of the original materials, and has also been named the Newe Inn, the Ounce and later the Catt (references to the white spotted leopards featured on the Dorset family coat of arms.)

In its heyday of coach travel there were an estimated 103 beds and 247 horses in the town – most of them at the Dorset.

It has been a centre of activity in the old High Street for nearly 400 years.

THOMAS SACKVILLE, EARL OF DORSET.
A FAMOUS STATESMAN.
M.P. FOR EAST GRINSTEAD, 1557. N. DANIELS,
STATIONER,

If these walls could speak...

This story is based on fact, but I have taken licence to expand its depth and warmth, because sometimes the truth is stranger than fiction.

It is dedicated to the following people:

Anne Tree
Wilfred Bumble
Miss Mary Sumner
Captain John Lancaster
Private Edward Jones

1247...

The moist sandy soil almost flew off the spade. Usually the digging and weeding of the large herb and vegetable garden, in the cleared dense woodland behind the alehouse, would be back-breaking work. Certainly, on the few local and scattered farms the soil was damp, thick and sticky blue clay, and the favoured conversation of the farmers who congregated by the smoky fire hearth was the hard work and toil needed to produce enough food to feed their animals, and themselves.

'Course, you chuck plenty 'o' shite on it,' said the oldest of the group, 'then you can' go wrong, seeing as them bloody swine and beast spend most of their days stuffing in one end, only to come spewing out t'other, bit like me kids. And me wife.......'

The grubby men laughed and one started to scratch his armpit and groin, his face etched with pleasure.

'Stop that ya dirty ol' fooker, you're like one of me bleeden pigs, only thems smell better than yous, and a lot prettier an' all.'

Seth Osborne sulked off, still scratching feverishly. His sharp, dirty fingernails tearing at his flesh, drawing blood. He could feel several large lumps under his armpit and groin which, sometimes in the night gave him little sleep as they throbbed and itched, almost driving him to tears. He headed towards the garden area where the young upstart Pip 'Digger' Harris was grafting.

'Rate you're going, you'll be on the other side of the land.' Seth mocked, trying to justify the cruel jokes from the farmers.

'As long as me lungs are full of God's air, the sun is shining and those dam swine don't piss on me radishes, I'm going to dig till me last breath.' He said as he heaved another shovelful of soft soil across the paddock.

The older man felt a sense of pride at the young lad's toil. Digger had transformed almost the whole area behind the long line of ramshackled, timber-framed buildings, from a wasteland to a Garden of Eden. Planting fruit trees in neat rows and keeping a small array of animals and beehives on the long stretches of land, chickens roamed clucking and several piglets scurried amongst the mud, the ale house's two black and white cats stood guard proudly, keeping the seeds and young plants safe from vermin attack.

It took up most of his days.

'They say good old King Henry III has granted the town a charter for a weekly market, every Monday, and with the annual fairs on the twenty-fourth and twenty-fifth of July.' Digger spoke with beaming enthusiasm, 'The lords of this town said I can sell me goods there, and keep twenty per cent of the profits. You may laugh old man…,' (Seth was too busy scratching to take notice) 'but I'm moving up and onwards….'

He enjoyed working on his own, but on some days several of the town girls would sit on a small bench and watch him. It made him uneasy because their whispers and giggles filled him with a strange sense of fascination: and lustful thoughts.

He'd been working the land for as long as he could remember, and having no family meant he'd been grafting to earn his keep and lodgings, a tidy hovel and with a large fireplace, from the age of seven. He had found a lump of sandstone, buried in the soil that was sort of head shaped, and he planned to carve the pretty face of his favourite girl and present it as a birthday gift: however he had still yet to start the masterpiece. It sat on a shelf in a cupboard, gathering dust.

His sweat had paid off now, as the owners of most of the town's better houses treated him well; in turn he provided fresh fruit and seasonal vegetables. Every Christmas he selected the most plumpest and white feathered goose for the dining table, and butchered the meat himself. Now at the age of nineteen, the years of digging and clearing gave his upper body and arms the size and strength of three men. A fact not unnoticed by the pretty girls nearby, whom every few minutes let out howls of laughter, and then sat tight-lipped and silent. Staring at the ground and twiddling their fingers in their hair.

'Shame you be wasting all that sweat and muscle on the land,' said Sally, the more confident and daring one, 'I can think of a lot better ways to put that to good use.' The girls muffled their rising hysterics.

'An' what be that then?' Digger said smiling.

One of the girls was sitting sideways on the bench, and as the cool summer breeze blew, her rough skirt lifted, revealing her smooth thighs and soft furry mound. Her bright eyes were as green as the new leaves that filled the trees.

He remembered the farmers laughing and telling him tales of such things, and the almost trance-like state a naked and pert young woman has on a man. He also remembered the advice that was handed down to him from the gaggle of beer swilling farmers and stable lads...

'Once you're up that tunnel of love, she'll have you down that church, and then it's a life of screaming babies, nagging and even more shite.'

'You can't beat the love of a good woman,' perked up another, 'waking up, all warm and hard.' The men had laughed again and ordered more ale from the bar.

'So tell me young lady.'

Sally was softly biting her bottom lip.

'What sorts of mischief you up to then,' Pip asked innocently, 'or do I have to spank the truth outa ya…'

He smiled at her, and then clapped his hands together loudly. The rooks in the top trees scattered. She squealed like a baby wild boar and gathered her long skirt around her knees, then stuck out her tongue and blew a loud raspberry.

'That's if you can catch me, or have you got no energy left, what with your digging and that, ha ha,' and started to scamper up towards the old High Street. The other girls sat open mouthed at her audacity and daring and then also ran off, giggling like silly bunnies.

Digger had also heard tales about the teasing and games these flighty minxes played. 'Best treat 'em mean, keep 'em keen,' was the standard old men's banter and he stopped chasing Sally, who was up on the higher terrace of the garden.

She blew another raspberry and shouted down to him. 'What's up with yous then, scaredy cat, scaredy cat,' and almost collapsed from running so fast.

'Well you young missy, I'll be tanning your hide before the sun's setting, you mark my words. You won't be able to sit down for a week when I've finished with ya,' he shouted back at her. Then he looked around, wondering what passers-by in the hollow lane next door might make of such conversation.

He started to laugh as Sally waved at him, giggled and turned around, lifted her skirt and flashed her round and pert bum. Then she disappeared into the smoky hovel.

He stood and thought for a moment, 'She'll be a fine lady one day. Crazy, but mighty fine,' and wandered back to his digging, his groin throbbed and his concentration was some-what displaced, blaming slight dizziness on the fact that it felt like every pint of blood in his body was racing towards his dick. 'And she has an arse like a peach,' he muttered as he plunged the spade into the soil with renewed and earnest vigour.

The name 'Grenest-ede', meaning 'a clearing in the forest' was changed to East Grenestede in the coming months, so as to distinguish it from another settlement further to the west. It also gave the town a hint of the future prosperity that beckoned. The market was growing in size and importance as farmers, tanners, coppers and traders in fine lace, silk and spices realised that over the last one hundred years, the four muddy tracks that lead to the town, several impassable in winter months, had now become well worn and deeply trodden gateways.

Not only was it a social and economic event, it brought people from all walks of life together, working hard at selling their goods, a vast array of specialist farm tools and exotic creatures: from mice to brightly coloured parrots. A gaggle of farm geese tottered through the high street in one long line, and a scruffy child wandered behind them with a small stick, chickens seem to be perched everywhere: clucking and preening themselves. On a nearby table other farm animals were being freshly butchered, and to the uninitiated the sight of steaming guts being scooped into copper vessels was quite a sight: and not for the squeamish. Wood pigeons, pheasants, ducks, squirrels and other game hung from wooden market stalls, festooned with meadow flowers and green branches: making people's mouths water. Sweet Chestnuts, hazels and walnuts grilled on small makeshift burners filling the air with blue smoke: and kippers, fresh perch and rainbow trout were also being smoked in short square boxes: Always, in the distance the gallows loomed.

The range and colours of apples on show took people's breath away, and huge clay and brick ovens baked vast quantities of fresh bread, the ovens being set up just behind the alehouse.

Scrawny Jack Tatty, the local thief, was again in the stocks. With his feet firmly clamped between two oak posts, his hands tied behind his back the children of the market traders taking it in turn to chuck rotting vegetables, eggs and apples at his defenceless head…! It caused great merriment.

And a few people arrived with half bricks, bottles and lumps of rough timber.

To the some of the gentle folk who lived in the town it was chaos. People shouting, drunkards staggering about with empty bottles proclaiming anything to anyone who would listen.

On one or more occasions the Ladies of the town would venture into the grubby streets, and witness the local village idiot pissing in a doorway: An old clay pipe clutched between his rotting teeth.

'Mornin ladies' he quipped whilst vigorously shaking his member: dotting the doorway with specks of foul dark yellow liquid.

The Ladies turned away, revolted as the acidic smell hurt their noses.

'Shall we get a nice side of pork to roast for Sunday? Asked one as they headed to the butcher's stall, 'And some nice fresh Bramleys for sauce? She added.

'Spectacular idea' said the other, still dabbing her face with a hankie.

They walked up to the butcher, whose huge grin and massive belly made them nervous.

'Mornin Ladies' he bellowed 'and what can I do for you today?

In one hand he had a plump goose, still alive. He held it firm and with the other took a mighty swoop with a razor sharp chopper, severing the birds head. In three more swift blasts he chopped off its legs, lower neck and split it straight down the middle, its guts spewing all over the table.

He then chucked the carcass over his back to a thin and grinning lad, who clutched a sharp knife with a menacing glint in his eyes.

'Whip its guts out will ya Spencer lad, and don't forget to wipe its arse an all' he roared 'These Ladies here look like they could do with fattening up eh? He then proceeded to laugh again and rub his monster belly.

As he turned around, the Ladies had gone...

'Oh well' he muttered: and grabbed another Goose from a wicker basket.

Some of the traders had competitions seeing who could shout the loudest to attract the most customers. Even making up little rhymes to amuse the wide eyed crowds.

'Buy your way to 'eaven, that comes to one groat 'n' seven: bless ya

Luv' Screamed Fat Pat the butcher, again rubbing his enormous stomach.

Slinky Thompson was having none of it...

'Goats milk 'n' cheese, if ya please, cash in the claw, cash on the nail, do me a deal 'n' I'll buy you 'n' ale' he belted out with a smug grin.

Tobias Moony, who had spent over a year travelling from

the Far East to trade, knew all the tricks…

'So who will buy a little bit of eastern promise then my love-lies?

With shameless showmanship he threw a deep burgundy blanket from his stool, and glittering rock gems and shinny trinkets dazzled people's eyes in the sunlight…

They flocked to see the strange shapes and bright colours, letting out 'Ohhing' and 'arring' sounds as they rubbed and inspected the unusual and exotic wears. Tobias stood tall and rubbed his hands with glee…

'Come come my friends; show me the colour of your money'

Fat Pat sniffed and grabbed another goose.

Alice Ragworthy, the local lace and boot string maker piped up…

'My good folk of Grinny, Don't listen to those clowns, their meat is old nags head, and should be run outa town' … the crowd began to applaud and whoop her up. She stood proud and looked around, nodding her head to the pleased and laughing mob…

'Now now boys, all's fair at the fair' she added… and winked.

It was all harmless fun, and they always ended up in the alehouse: getting rather drunk and cracking rude jokes until they were thrown out at some un-Godly hour.

A small group of mud and horse-poo splattered children sat in a circle next to a blazing log burner… singing rhymes…

'Ringa ringa roses, a pocket full of posers, atissoo, atisso, we all fall down'. And burst into giggles.

All except the woodman's sickly and blurry eyed son, who kept scratching his arm pits, looking around to see if anyone noticed.

On his cheek a large dark red/black blister had begun to throb and pustulate…

Even the ramshackle and wonky old timber-framed ale house was attracting more discerning customers, inspiring the friendly manager and his large hilarious wife to dress in a manner more suitable.

Wiping the bar she spoke loudly so all and sundry could hear. 'I've even got the old goat to stop picking his nose and scratching his balls as he pulls yer pints,' she said, mocking faint disgust.

'That be all well and good, and bless ye, my little bubbly cess-pit, best not to tell what you put in them meat pies of yours.'

Farmer Wilmington spluttered on his pint, 'I'll swear last time I bit into one of 'em, it mooed.'

They all laughed as Digger walked into the bar. He had heard the conversation from outside and calmly announced,

'Only the choicest chunks, eh Molly? Eyelash, foreskin and minced bladders? Lovely, I'll be ordering one of them for me dinner then and wash it down with some of that fine ale. Now where's that Sally be hiding? Me and her have some unfinished business.'

He winked at Molly, who, with a typical mother's instinct, scolded his impertinence, wagging her plump fingers at him and muttering 'You be keeping your grubby paws to yourself young man. She be turning eighteen this year and what with some of the fine gentlemen now frequenting our establishment, I be seeing her going up in the world.'

Wilmington perked up and spoke through tight lips,

'I be seeing her spending all her time going down, or on all fours, you be getting my drift,' he winked at the now crowded bar. Molly joined in the laughter and then scolded the whole motley crew.

'You be nothing but a load of randy old dogs. Supp your ales and button it, my little princess shouldn't be within earshot of your filthy minds.'

Sally was sitting just around the corner on the stairs stroking one of the cats: her mouth formed a minx-like grin, her green eyes sparkled and a large damp patch was forming on her skirt where she sat.

The fine gentlemen Molly was referring to were the sons of the wealthy merchants that had started to build and reconstruct most of the tatty and leaning-over Hall houses that ran in almost a complete unbroken line on the town's south side. They were not liked by the simple and hard working folk in and around the town; their arrogance and brash attitude especially annoyed the local peasant farmers.

Ernie 'the Beacon' Warren spoke, the appropriate nickname was affectionately given to him by Molly: mainly because of his bright red and bulbous nose… as he had spent years as a prize fighter in the nearby hamlet of Hartfeild.

'Those shite bags strut about this town like they own it' he scorned'

'They bloody well do, most of it anyway' said Molly laughing.

'I mean, just because your rich daddy pays for everything, don't give no-one the right to be an arrogant prick, There be a great change in the air, you mark my words'.

'Wouldn't know what a hard day's hard graft is…' he continued before gulping his pint down in one, and crackling his fingers.

Only last week several of the 'jumped up pounces' as Wilmington called them, came swaggering into the ale house, turning up their noses at the sawdust on the floor, the tatty ale tankards and mocking aloud Sally, who was vigorously polishing the brass and old farm implements by the fireplace.

'I say, peasant girl.' He spat on his leather shoe. 'I'll give you a silver coin to clean the muck from my footwear.'

Sally looked confused and turned to Molly for guidance, who kindly beckoned the young gentleman over.

'Well young squire, I'll be happy to give you a pot of gold... if you kiss my big round arse.'

And she delicately blinked her eyelids at him and his flounce-attired cronies, who, caught off guard by such honesty and integrity, slipped out the front doors in silence.

The whole bar erupted into gales of laughter. Molly stood proud with her hands on both hips and pushed out her chest.

'Bleeden peasant girl. They wouldn't know a princess if they saw one,' and opened her arms, went up to Sally and hugged her hard.

'Promise me girl, you don't go near that lot of stuck up dandies, you promise now.'

Sally looked confused and nodded her head

'They may talk proper an' all that, with their fancy clothes and pappy's money, but they have the manners of bog rats and are just such arrogant weasels.'

As the evening came to a close the motley crew all shook hands, Molly smiled warmly and pushed out her ample chest again. Wilmington couldn't resist.....

'So, if we all chip in together and find that pot of gold.' She knew what was coming. 'Any chance like we can all kiss y...?'

'Get outa here ya dogs, haven't you got ya beast and swine to tend to?' and slapped all the men's heads as they sauntered out the back doors, one at a time. As her hand swacked Willmy, he did his puppy dog eyes,

'That's no way to talk about the wife and kids' He said and raucous laughter followed them all down the hollow lane home.

Lady Stefani van Glendyne watched as the young man panted, sweated and cursed as he dug around the old tree stump, kicking it with his foot and muttering 'bastad, ya fooken bastad,' then reeling in agony as the pain shot up his leg.

'You total fooken bastad.' he screamed again, hopping around the Portlands, cursing like a madman. Chickens scattered and pigs snorted, their happy faces almost smiling. The cats ran and hid behind a holly bush.

'What you laughing at porky? Any more of ya cheek and you'll be bacon rashers and stew long before Christmas.' Porky tottered off to find a big pile of shit to play in.

'Yeah that's it, go on......apple sauce, apple sauce,' he muttered as Porky wallowed in the mud and almost grinned.

She had been looking around the new area after her parents had moved to a big and grand house just outside town. The streets were quite grubby she noticed, but it was better than the cramped and ill-aired London town. Her father ranted on about some De Montfort fellow stirring up trouble, and the general political unrest and back stabbing that ruled their city lives.

At least now in the country air and freshness, a slower pace of life could resume. Or so she thought.

Peering around a large oak tree she watched the strong and funny man as he shouted at the pigs, and cursed the tree stump, and muttered 'apple sauce'.

'Must be these country folk,' she thought, 'be a bit soft in the head.'

He had taken off his shirt and his body glistened with sweat, and she felt a funny tingle happening between her legs and squeezed them together tightly. Closing her eyes she imagined his hard body pushing her around, tugging her hair and ....

'You alright there missy?'

Her eyes shot open and she looked to the ground.

'Well, err... Yes. Yes of course. I was just searching for some lemon grass, for that foot of yours, works wonders as pain relief.'

She stood up proudly. 'There, see I found some.'

Much to her acute relief there was a small patch in the herb garden, and she rushed over and grabbed a handful and began to scrunch it up and prepare the remedy.

'Give me your foot, now you silly man. What sort of person shouts at pigs?' She started the conversation as if she had known him all her life. 'And calls them apple sauce.' she laughed, and blushed.

'Well you think that's barmy, but when farmer Wilmington gets pissed off at a still born lamb, he shouts at the mamma sheep 'mint sauce, mint sauce'.'

They both laughed out loud.

'You're all crackers down here. There, how's that feel?'

The pain had gone and he was looking right into her eyes, his hand touched hers and a jolt of tingling pleasure coursed through their bodies.

She lunged at him, pressing her lips to his and clawing his body. In response he picked her up in one swoop, and lips still locked, carried her to the old barn. He kicked open the door, threw her onto the soft hay and ripped the rest of their clothes off, and went at it like wild beasts.

With one hand steadying his ferocious thrusts and the other grabbing her long hair as she let out little gasps, then a low moan and then began to almost scream.

Sally came skipping down the wonky old path, in one hand a small wooden tray with a tankard of home made lemonade and honey-soaked oatmeal biscuits, with the other she tidied her hair and skirt, gently humming to her self. Her minx-like grin returned and her eyes sparkled as she saw Digger's shirt by the barn door.

Then she heard the screams. Alarmed at first but, as curiosity replaced panic, she moved the barn door, which was almost off its hinges. She peered inside.

All she saw was a thrashing and writhing mass of human flesh, legs and arms entangled; hair and sweat entwined. The girl was now on all fours with eyes wild and howling like a wolf, and Digger was with his teeth clenched, and eyes shut, with one foot firmly wedged on a floor beam to stop him from falling over as they both shuddered and came together.

Sally dropped the tray on the soft hay and ran up to the alehouse, tears streaming down her face as she sobbed uncontrollably.

As the months passed into winter, he wondered why he never saw the lady again. The 'dandies' had returned every now and then to the ale house, looking around suspiciously in every nook and cranny.

Sally never spoke to him, and he wondered if someone might have seen or heard the barn liaison. If she did look at him it was with hate and tear-filled eyes.

The following spring began as per norm, and Digger had built a massive fire at the bottom of the Portlands, heaving up masses of branches and trees with a pitched fork, clearing even more land for crop growing. Ghostly white smoke plumed into the air, almost like large clouds they rose up into the dense trees: slithers of sunlight pierced through, almost cutting sharp shards of pointed light.

Digger stood and watched for a minute. Even though he had spent most of his working life outside there was something still so spectacular about the way nature's colours and smells, patterns and landscapes filled his life. He remembered last spring watching fox cubs leaping about like small kittens, hearing grumpy baby birds shrieking as the mother brought a tasty worm for breakfast. One had jumped in the nest so frantically it had fallen out and sat on the grass looking dazed and confused. As Digger leaned down to picked it up, its mouth started opening and closing, as if expecting food. Its beady eyes staring at him intensely.

'Well I could let you have some of me bread and cheese little fella' he said, beginning to climb the tree and replace the roughed-up little ball of fluff with its brothers and sisters,

'But your mama might just give a me a good scolding for me good deed' he laughed.

As he spoke the mother bird flew right past his head and let out a long chattering blast….then perched herself on a nearby branch, still yakking and flapping her wings about.

'Keep your blooming feathers on' and copied the bird's movements.

He smiled at the mother, all huffy and flappy.

'spose I could always let Mr Fox have your youngen for his breakfast then,' as he put the baby back. The other's mouths started their feeding pattern, their tiny yellow beaks gawping.

When he climbed back down the tree the mother flew straight to the nest and looked back at him…. Her small black eyes glaring yet desperate.

There was a certain view, through a gap in the hedge that looked out across the sunken meadows. As the spring turned to summer the stable horses grazed out side at night, and in the mornings after a quick gallop around the paddocks their necks and backs let off great rising pockets of sweat. On some mornings the mist had settleled about 3 yards above the ground; it appeared that the horses had no legs and the vapour from their backs gave them a really odd appearance. Almost like ghosts.

He remembered trying to tell the pub people of such a description, but as usual Wilmington had laughed out loud.

'You been on that ale for breakfast then me laddie? Ghost horses my arse'.

There were many times in his days when nature's splendour and almost perfect sense of equilibrium sent shivers down his spine, and he was so glad he was not stuck in the Smokey town by a market stool, or had to stand in the new buildings, whose newly designed fronts were like wooden boxes.

As the blaze took hold he noticed several smartly dressed men heading down the path, and felt confident that they wanted more work done.

'You, I say, you boy.' The older-looking gang of five men pointed and rushed at him. Taken aback as they grabbed his arms and held him in a tight grip.

'If you got some sort of problem,' Digger spoke, 'then let's sort it man to man.' He was unafraid of conflict.

One of the men swung a large heavy tool handle, which thudded into Digger's stomach, sending him sprawling to the floor. Winded and flat out he looked up.

'You don't work that way now do ya, fooken yellow bellied scum. Yous juss cowards, thass all...'

With his breath gone, the hired thugs ensured a savage beating, kicking his head and ribs with great repetition. It did not stop for seven minutes. Digger passed out after four and his limp and broken body was unrecognisable as a human being. The five men were panting as great hues of breath streamed from their lungs.

'That'll teach the dirty fucker,' and spat on the lifeless corpse.

'Get his legs, come on, move it, move it.'

Three of the men picked up the body and, with a swinging motion and a count of three, heaved Digger onto the fire. He landed directly in the middle and the heat and flames soon consumed his flesh.

The men almost marched to the ale house and on reaching inside, one yelled, 'Steffy, get in here now.'

She appeared at the front doors, in her arms a small gargling bundle was held close to her body. The older man snatched the baby and without any compassion thrust it into Molly's bewildered arms.

'If that dirty pig fucker can't keep his dick in his trousers, soiling our family's good name and seducing our beloved sister into a brazen hussy, then you keep and pay for the bastard son.'

He was spitting with rage, as he grabbed the girl almost by the throat and marched out the doors in silence. The rest of the men followed, scowling at the peaceful and gentle folk.

There was silence for what seemed hours, and then Molly spoke,

'Well blow me down with a feather; he's a bonny little chap.'

The baby gurgled, squealed and then did a bubbly fart. Molly tried to ease the tension, 'Sure 'ees not yours Wilmy, after that little display? Bless the little fella's cotton socks, and he's got Digger's nose. Where is he anyway?'

Weeks passed and no sign of Digger could be found. His tools still lay where he was working that day. Most assumed he had moved on, being a free sprit and now in demand from the surrounding villages for his digging abilities.

Sally took control of the baby, a deep resentment building and burning her insides every minute that passed. She often left the baby crying and hungry, as if justifying the pain of what she saw that day in the barn.

She could take it no more, and in the highest room of the alehouse she prepared herself. Taking the baby completely covered in bundles of cloth, she slipped her hands onto the small soft body, prayed, pushed down hard and waited for silence. Molly was watching her intensely through a large crack in one of the doors.

When the little bundle stopped moving, she crawled across the highest beams and placed the limp package in a small crevice behind the main chimney stack. Covering it in small rocks and soot she calmly went back down the stairs. She had already prepared a small box, and with genuine tears of guilt announced.

'The baby's died. It just went blue and died.' She began sobbing and broke down.

'There, there, my precious, easy come easy go they say.'

Molly was smiling softly. The baby was safe and snug in the stable buildings, with Wilmington in charge and pulling silly faces and making mooing sounds, which made it gurgle and giggle with delight.

And no-one would miss just one piglet.

They held a small service in the gardens, at 10.00am, with Sally weeping, Wilmington looking bored, and the rest of the ale house locals muttering quiet prayers for the little fella. The green leaves on the trees reached and brushed against each other, in silence. One large beech tree, its huge bows stretching out like greying skeletal arms lurked amid the neatly cropped hedges: a slight breeze made the tiny finger like branches rustle and dance.

They dug a deep hole, right next to where Digger had been beaten and thrown on the fire and placed the tiny wooden box gently to rest.

Within three months Sally had met and married a very wealthy local merchant thirty years her senior, and took up residence in a fine and grand house by the gateway of the soon to be named Lancaster Great Park. He died, leaving Sally one of the wealthiest women in Sussex, after a bitter cold winter that claimed many lives.

At the grand old age of thirty-six, Sally was finding the big house a bore, but she enjoyed the garden, especially growing fruit trees and herbs. She now found it backbreaking work and sought the labour of a keen and fit young man from the town: whose reputation for hard work and polite manners was the talk of the ladies tea parties.

He started work the following week and Sally's knees went to jelly as she looked out of one of the top windows. The man was working with his shirt off, and the muscled contours of his back and movements as he thrust the spade into the soil made her gasp. She wandered down to the garden; her breath in short pants and called to him. As he turned around and smiled she almost passed out.

'Morning Madam, be a good day for digging, the soil here is very good.'

His face, as he spoke, was so familiar and he gestured with his

Rough hands about the rows of fruit trees and herbs she had planted.

'You be quite keen for this gardening lark, for a woman like. Didn't think you ladies 'ad it in ya.' He winked at her with a saucy grin; and his bright green eyes sparkled with passion and fire.

With trembling lips Sally asked him more questions, which he answered with one word, either a 'yep', or a 'nope'.

'All you need to know missy, is the name's Digger. Never knew me parents, never trust no-one, and some of that home-made lemonade and honey oatmeal biscuits wouldn't go amiss...what ya say then girl?'

'But I ...I... This cannot be. I....I.'

Sally's mind went back to that night in the attic and the baby.

'Speak up there missy; pig got ya tongue or summat?'

She then realised who he was.

In the Portlands behind the alehouse, Porky was sniffing and rummaging by the remains of a large fire, and as his blackened snout schooved through the ash, the charred remains of

Digger's foot came unearthed. He nudged it across the meadow to where apples had fallen and began a feast fit for a king.

Pigeons began a nesting frenzy in the gutters and hoppers, and rooks took charge of the chimneys pots, their harsh and cruel 'caw caw' callings seemed a dark and evil warning to the subtle 'Coo Coo' of the timid pigeons, who hid in fear of the large, ferocious black feathered, beady eyed demons.

The alehouse was closed down and boarded up, and teams of grubby men smashed and pulled the entire structure to the ground. One of the largest chimney stacks came crashing through the old timbers and roof tiles, and a massive cloud of dust rose, swirled about and then floated off over the Portlands, covering most of the fresh green leaves with a fine and white/grey dust. Most of the long beams were salvaged to be re-used, but no one touched the long Portlands, especially the one behind the alehouse for nearly 100 years.

From the church across the road, a single bell chimed.

There was a deep sense of change in the air.

Porky

1990...

Steve Spiller cursed loudly, almost shouting at himself. 'Where's the bloody hammer now?'

He had just nailed six large sheets of plywood to batons to create a smaller but warmer bathroom. His hair was full of dust and dead pigeon feathers; occasionally he found one, curled up in a ball: it's white and perfectly formed bones almost model like. He was in the attic flat above the Dorset Arms and the insulation was non existent. The hammer was in the cellar. And there was always that strange smell in the roof space, almost like, he felt silly saying it 'babies'.

He walked down to the cellar almost trance-like and, sure enough, there was the hammer on a barrel, near the chimney stack foundations, covered in dust.

He spent most weekends at the pub, and the evenings too. A new manager had taken over after the establishment was sold to the first private consortium of owners since 1912.

The now delicious orange/red and jet black mirrored interiors, remnants of its days as a 'Bernie Inn' from the 1970's still stood loud and proud, with every chair, table and surface painted bright red. The carpet was enough to make people dizzy, with long amber and yellow stripes, the company's logo emblazoned in uncoordinated splurges of crimson and green and ill-looking plastic plants hung like limp lettuces from grubby Roman planters.

'The whole place looks like a bloody Chinese knocking shop,' said the manager, shaking his head and wondering why he didn't inspect the pub, especially the first-floor restaurant, in much finer detail.

'Probably take more money if it was.' Steve giggled and started to laugh, 'Mind you, I don't know what the council would say about that one.'

'Probably be right up for it,' said John, the new manager and also started to laugh. 'Can you imagine? Ahh, Councillor

Smyth, we have a large range of Indian, Chinese, Thai or full English, and the food's not bad either. Will you be requiring spanking or non-spanking?'

They both laughed loudly.

'I'm thinking what this place needs is a bloody great skip and a bit of hard work, I'll draw up some plans for the Monday morning meeting.'

Steve's main job there, for a small fee of free drinks after work, more often than not half a bottle of Pernod, was to re-route most of the older electric cables, and to strip the walls, floors and doors of their ghastly and vulgar attire.

The pub had a steady evening trade, but was very quiet most days. Some evenings there were more staff than customers. The busy trade from the long stretch of ugly and totally inappropriate office blocks in Cantelupe Road had almost stopped. The rents were so high most local businesses relocated to nearby Crawley new town where you could get twice the space for half the cost.

The old market was obliterated, rendering half the road a ghastly reminder of the 1980's lust for profit over people. It now sat empty and vandalised whilst the local bigwigs made plans to build another 4,000 houses on green belt land.

The plans for the pub were approved and the idea was to recreate the atmosphere of an olde country pub. Orange was replaced with subtle greens, reds disposed of in place of warm browns and rough sawn timber was nailed half way up the walls. Light bulbs were switched to a lower wattage to soften the mood.

As the work progressed, Steve spent a lot of time in the pub alone. It closed at 2.30 pm to reopen at 6.00 pm everyday, so most of the work was done at this time. But every time he was in the manager's flat at the top of the building that horrible smell would be in the air.

'Have you noticed that weird smell, John, in the flat? It's like sweet sickly yucky..... yucceeeecc...'

Steve turned up his face as just the thought of it made him want to vomit.

'It stinks like babies, you know when they crap and stuff.'

John let out a huge laugh, 'You're going soft. I've never experienced that one you nutter. Keep off that Pernod, it's rotting your brain.'

'I've left plenty of screaming boomers in the pan a few times, that's enough to make your eyes water and the wallpaper peel, but babies.... You're off your head mate.'

The manager was going away for the weekend, to meet up with his girlfriend, and hire a van to pick up the furniture from their house by the coast. They closed the pub so Steve could get on with ripping up the old nasty carpets throughout the building and smash a few walls about here and there. The light fittings in the whole building looked like they were from the 1920's so they had to go.

After sinking his fourth glass of Pernod and turning off all the lights downstairs, he headed to the top flat to continue the renovations and as he walked up the stairs the smell hit him.

'Bloody hell, it's getting worse...' And felt a surge of nausea.

He'd brought some air freshener from the bar and sprayed the place from top to bottom, gagging as the reek of patchouli and lemongrass, mixed with the essence of baby's crap, filled the small rooms.

The town was oddly quiet and as he heard the bells across the road chime out at 10.00 pm the whole place seemed deathly still.

His ears twitched in the dark, as he'd had to shut off all the power and stumble around with a torch, which every now and then just stopped working.

Then he heard it, a baby crying.

It started like a small wail, and as he rushed around the flat looking up at the ceilings and opening cupboards it grew in volume. In one cupboard a large piece of head-shaped sandstone sat on the shelf: He remembered clearing it out last week, putting the stone in a black sack and dropping it from one of the top flat windows. It made a sickening crash into the metal bins below. He also remembered the same stone was in one of the cellar cupboards last week, and months ago it was found in the stable flat, under the kitchen sink. The wailing was now driving him mad and he climbed up the metal ladders to the roof space where it seemed to be coming from.

The torch beam shone like a long thin white tunnel, dust and cobwebs were floating in the air. It was cold and the noise had reduced itself to a tiny gurgle. He scanned the roof beams and as the light fixed on one of the chimney stacks, a movement caught his eye. He had to crawl on all fours to get closer as dust and dirt filled his mouth. The noise and smell was definitely coming from behind the stack.

The torch flickered off and he cursed as he slipped off one of the beams, cracking his head as he regained balance.

'Fuck it...'

A loud cry pierced his ears and panic filled every sense, the torch flickered on again and he crouched down and looked at what appeared to be an old bundle of rags, covered in soot.

There was a jerky movement from the rags and his heart missed four beats, his mouth went dry and he reached out and grabbed a piece of tatty roof batten and poked the bundle.

The noise stopped.

'Probably a rat's nest,' he thought and, in revulsion, pushed the bundle up and over the brickwork. As it landed on the sooty floor he used the stick to unravel the rags, and give whatever monster was lurking there a hefty thwack.

The smell vanished and on pulling open the package tiny bits of white bone appeared. Then a skull.

A whole complete skeleton was wrapped up in the rag, and he shone the torch at the find. Clambering on both knees he peered at the bones, they were not human. The skull was long and animal looking; it had small bright white teeth and each of the minute ribs was so delicate and precise. He noticed on one side of the rib cage a slight indent, like a pressure had been applied, causing several of the ribs to break. It wasn't a cat or dog, and too big for a rat.

'At least it's not a bloody baby,' he said laughing with relief.

The torch dimmed, and then flickered off.

The following morning he headed to the town's library, and picked out several books on animal anatomy, scouring the pages of skeletons and bones, keeping a mental picture of the remains firmly in his mind.

One picture struck him; it stood out on the page. It was a picture of a piglet. Nervously he turned to the next, and there it was. What he had found in the attic was a complete skeleton of a young piglet.

John knew something was up when he came through the door the next day, fearing a flood or fire judging by the serious face on Steve.

'You look like you've seen a ghost,' he said, 'I've heard all the stories,' and slapped him on the back.

'You better come and have a look at this.'

He was so stern as he led John up the stairs, up the metal ladder and shone the torch into the darkness.

'Over there.' The beam of light fell onto the area of the find.

'What? Yeah, yeah, it's a chimney. Whoopee doo do.'

'Look at those rags, just down there.'

He wiggled the beam in frustration and John leant over by the chimney and pulled out the bundle, lifted it up and shook it.

Dust, cobwebs and brick rubble fell onto the floor. The rags were empty.

'Mate, you got to leave that Pernod alone, it's fuzzed your brain.' John laughed and tossed the rags back behind the stack.

'So you found a bunch of old rags, at least you might have discovered some money or jewels, or treasure.'

Steve stood open-mouthed, 'But I found a....' he felt very stupid saying it.

'A what, elephant, a whale, a wasp's nest?'

'No, a...' He couldn't say it.

'The four apocalyptic horsemen, an old granny...?'

'Don't take the piss.' He felt totally stupid saying it. 'It was a piglet skeleton.'

'You what? A flaming piglet skeleton? In the roof? In this building? Right here? Mate, are you on drugs?'

'No...no, yesterday... I found it. Right there. I did some re-search at the library this morning. It was a piglet, I found a bloody piglet.'

'So where it is then, scampered off to market?'

Steve turned off the torch, feeling really dumb and quite numb. He climbed down the ladder and headed to the bar. He heard John laughing uncontrollably and singing, 'This little piggy went to market, this lit...'

Pouring a large glass of Pernod with ice and blackcurrant he sat on one of the chairs.

'But I saw a bloody piglet.' He downed the glass. 'But I saw a bloody piglet.'

He made John swear to keep "his little find" a secret, but on some days the urge was almost uncontrollable.

'Wanna bacon sandwich Steve?' laughed John, as the new staff looked on puzzled. 'There's that show on telly tonight, you know, only fools and horses, them Trotter boys eh?'

Steve groaned, and put his head in his hands.

    'Better start training the girls with these new tills; don't want them making a pig's ear of it.'

    'Bastard,' Steve muttered, contemplating giving up the Pernod for good.

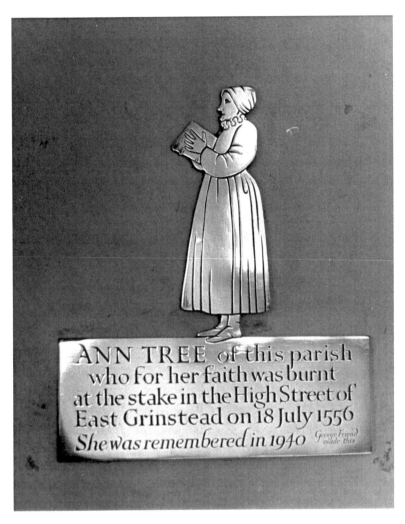

ANN TREE of this parish who for her faith was burnt at the stake in the High Street of East Grinstead on 18 July 1556 She was remembered in 1940 *George Friend made this*

1556...

Anne Tree gently tied the rough string around another bunch of English herbs – parsley, sage, rosemary and thyme. In her large wicker basket were apples stored from the autumn, and cherries of such deep purple they looked like the eyes of the deer roaming across the forest.

Her cottage near East Grinstead, at the bottom of a steep hollow, was small but filled with treasure, her treasure.

Even though her timber framed and crocked old home was crammed with pots and baskets, outside in her garden nature flourished in a spectacular display of colour and texture. Every single one of the plants, trees and flowers in large clumps had their own special medical properties, and she nurtured them with a mother's care.

Dense shaggy bushes of Camomile, with their bright white smiling flowers could be crushed and used as an antispasmodic, disinfectant and anti-inflammatory treatment, Lavender was used for headaches, insomnia, melancholia and bronchial-asthma.

Lady's Mantle, one of her most popular remedies could be infused with warm goat's milk and soothed women's menstrual troubles, and gave great ease and comfort to the pains of childbirth.

Wild Fennel was used to improve eyesight, Pumpkin flesh and seeds contained many healing minerals, and summer and winter Jasmine accelerated the metabolism, improving blood circulation and was commonly know for its aphrodisiac effects: Many an old gentleman would knock on Anne's door in the still of the night, hunching silently by the entrance, waiting for Anne to bring the magic potion that would restore virility and stamina, so his younger and eager wife could be satisfied and fulfilled in the bedroom department.

She always gave them a knowing little smile and a nod as they slipped silver coins into her hand, and then scuttled off into the night.

Around the old and gracious cherry trees wild strawberries grew in abundance, their sharp red juice administered three times a day brought much relief to rheumatism, gout and had magnificent detoxifying properties: Even the batch of unruly stinging nettles at the bottom of the garden had a purpose, the leaves could be placed on the bare skin just above any vital organ. It was an uncomfortable process but as the stings produced large red rashes and white bumps it also stimulated blood flow to the organ, greatly improving its function and efficiency.

She had never married, enjoying her own company to that of the roughness and crudity of the local men. Her wonky old black cat, with one eye missing because the dirty children that hung around the hollow after dark threw stones at it, hissed through their teeth 'witch, witch, here comes the old witch...'

She said that she did not attend the Catholic services at the church as she did not understand Latin. That and the freezing cold seats played havoc with her hips and knees. She made a tidy living from supplying herbs, fruit and potions to the workers at the big alehouse on the corner of the High Street. They always gave her a warm welcome and a cup of brandy tea on cold days, for more often than not she had some magic tonic in her basket.

'God 'elp me Anne, it's me guts. Rumbling like a storm all night. Been sitting on the pan pushing like it's me last breath, nothing's come out but half me tubes.'

The people in the kitchen of the house all looked at each other, wincing as they imagined such a sight, and poor old John's bright red face with his cheeks all puffed up and eyes bulging.

'Feels like me insides are trying to get out,' he said wheezing.

'We'll 'ave you sorted in no time Johnny boy,' she said, reaching into her formidable basket of hidden depths. The onlookers craned their necks as if to see from where the magic came. She pulled out some blackened seedpods and, with time-learned skill, crushed them quickly into a thick paste and added some honey.

'Get that down ya, and get yourself off to the men's room, sharpish,' she smiled. The pods were pure senna seeds...

'That lot could clear the drains of this whole land,' she laughed with a sympathetic grin.

Johnny trudged off clutching his backside as if to hold in what was left of his guts and, as he disappeared around the door, a large gurgle and a soft squeaky sound followed him, almost like someone shutting a small door.

'Ooh my Lord, what the....'

The kitchen staff and Anne roared with laughter as the noises omitted from the small brick lav echoed around the building.

Johnny played up his condition – blowing loud raspberries with his tongue off the back of his hand.

'Sweet Jesus, she's coming through.'

He picked up a small piece of rock and dropped it into the bucket, careful to avoid a splashback...pladoumph....

'Oh my word, it's a girl... she's beautiful.'

He heard the others roar again, and started to chuckle to himself.

'Poor old bastard,' said Thomas Dungate, the kitchen cleaner. 'He's on that sea-food diet.'

The staff chuckled like giggly children.

'He sees food and bloody well eats it.'

By now Anne's sides were hurting, tears were streaming down her face, and the whole place was filled with laughter. Johnny emerged from the bucket room, panting.

'Bless the Lord, Anne; you are indeed an angel, that's the best part of me gone.'

'You've lost some weight there John,' said Thomas. 'You'll be wearing last year's trousers at this rate...'

Suddenly there was an ear-bursting thwack. The manager of the olde inn had smashed a thick cane across one of the dense wooden tables.

'What be this ... What be this witchcraft going on? Taking the Lord's name in vain ... You'll pay for this blasphemous treachery.'

The younger members of staff scurried off into the darkness. Anne, Thomas and Johnny stood trembling in front of the man in black. He beckoned in five burly soldiers who trussed up the three bemused friends, the tears of laughter still stinging Anne's eyes. They were dragged to the dark cellar and chained to the walls like animals. Johnny let off a massive blast of wind, his gut rumbling in fear and confusion.

There was a trial, which lasted two minutes. With his eyes wide and rolling around their sockets, the preacher screamed from the pulpit, pointing to the condemned '...and God shall burn those souls who torment His name, and cast the dark shadow of witchcraft to this land.' The small crowd jeered and hissed at the terrified friends. Anne opened her mouth to speak...

'We did not intend to...'

A loutish guard slapped her hard across the face.

'Silence woman,' the preacher bellowed, 'you have no say in this matter.' His face contorted with rage and hate. Johnny's wind let rip once more.

'Remove these animals. Let them feel God's wrath in all its glory... Amen.'

The shaking crowd nodded their heads, obedient and almost silent; they mooched off ... 'Amen'.

The eighteenth of July was market day. Crowds gathered and sniffed, prodded and rummaged amongst the large selection of goods filling the makeshift tables and stools in the bright sun. The warm air smelt of chestnuts, stewed cooking apples and horse dung, which littered around the streets in big steaming piles.

'Be a good day for a burn'en,' said one of the local girls who worked at the alehouse, munching on a bag of cherries and spitting the pips at the foot of the mass of rolled-up twigs, branches and oak logs piled high. Three tall stakes towered into the sky with chains reflecting on the silver armour of the soldiers who stood nearby. Their stern faces and stance adding to the spectacle and theatre of it all.

The olde inn manager lurked in the shadows. After the burning business would be booming and in preparation he had named a local ale 'Martyrs' choice'.

'Bound to sell well,' he smirked, 'people's throats being dry an' that...'

The preacher appeared from the baying crowd, his nostrils bellowing with pride and importance. Small blond boys clung to his robe, looking up in awe, and several young girls fainted, to be carted off and splashed with water. He stood on the steps outside the large oak-framed buildings, looking around the silent crowd. The church bell rang ten times, each ring seemingly getting louder as the tension grew to almost beyond hysteria.

'Bring forth the heretics' he screamed.

The crowd cheered as Anne and the others were dragged from the dark cellars. All their hair has been shaved and, wearing just white hessian robes, they staggered to the stakes. Anne looked around. Although most of the crowd's faces were a seething mass of hate, with the preacher standing with his arms outstretched towards the bell tower, she could see people she knew, their eyes darted away from hers as if in shame and disbelief. As the cold steel chains were fastened, Johnny let rip. As he did so his face swelled up and he slumped against Thomas, drool running down his cheek. His heart had given way and only the harsh chains held him up. The crowd let out a loud booing sound and started throwing apples and cherries at his blueing face ... his eyes still open.

As the smoke started to rise and the heat began to grow, Anne lost sight of the crowd. She could see the preacher whooping up the spectators, reading aloud pieces from the Bible, all in Latin. A gang of small urchins stood as near as possible to the flames, gawping up at her with snotty noses running, poking the growing furnace with long sticks and giggling.

'It's just a game to them' she thought. 'Such innocent hearts and minds, wide open the filth and depravity of evil and corrupt men.'

When the smoke cleared as the flames grew hotter she saw two small girls, holding hands. They were twins in matching cloths, with identical long auburn hair and pale white skin. They were both just staring at Anne, quite expressionless. She tried to ignore the rising agony as the flames got closer and smiled at them; her bottom lip began to bleed as her teeth almost cut it in half. Both the girls smiled back, and waved with their tiny hands. Suddenly a smartly dressed woman dragged the girls away, scolding them openly and pointing at Anne, shaking her head and glaring in disgust. They were then tugged off into the ugly crowd. Anne took a deep breath, held it, and then took another. Starving her brain of oxygen as she breathed out deeply several more times, the tips of her fingers were melting, her toes were just burnt charcoal stubs and her eyes felt they were going to burst: even the tears running down her face evaporated as the unforgiving heat and flames licked and clawed at her now naked flesh. She slipped into a coma, only vaguely hearing the screams of Thomas as his robe flashed into an orange ball of flame.

In the bar the only talking point was the disappointment of the burnings...

'Nice sunny day an' all, they should have been wriggling for hours. It's much better when it rains.' laughed the manager, wiping the bar. 'So, who's for another Martyr's then?

He looked around, and saw a child playing with a grubby doll. She had made a small noose and was dangling the doll by its neck, and making crackling noises.

Just then, the Preacher came through the door, looking very proud of himself and aloof...

'Ahhhh preacher ... the usual is it?'

1912...

The soft gentle rain hovered in the air, almost invisible. It created a haze across the churchyard, making the tombstones appear like greying loose teeth.

The vicar's wife hurried across the cobblestone path to the shop, she was making cakes today in readiness for the annual May Fair in a few weeks' time. As she approached the town entrance to the graveyard, she noticed the three inscribed slabs on the right. Although the rain was not heavy, it had soaked the grass and her feet, but the slabs were dry, and as the rain landed it hissed and evaporated and small puffs of steam swirled off in every direction. It was 9.56 in the morning and, looking up at the tower as if to seek an explanation, it puzzled her as to why. She reached down and ran her hand over the hard dry stones, then, yelping like a pup, she pulled her hand away – the gravestones were almost red hot. Three red welts grew suddenly on her hand and almost anger swept over her.

She began to sweat profusely. Composing herself she read the writing on the stones:

Thomas Dungate   Anne Tree   John Forman

The names made her shiver. 'Poor souls,' she thought. She looked up at the tower once more to check the time. The clock shuddered and ten chimes rang out. She shivered again and, remembering the pain in her hand, looked at her palm.

The welts were gone; there was no pain, but what shook her more was that, in the distance three dark figures lurked in the corner of the churchyard. They seemed to be looking directly at her, even though she could not see their faces. Blaming last night's glass of red wine on causing such an illusion, she almost ran the remaining twenty yards towards the shops.

There was a huge commotion going on in the town centre. Heavy digging equipment and scores of grubby men in overcoats were hanging around. In the middle of them was a short, round man, barking orders and pointing in all directions.

'What occurs?' she asked two old ladies politely.

'They're resurfacing the old road,' one replied.

'Been a while,' said the other.

'Yesss,' they both said at the same and started tutting in unison.

'And all this machinery. So much noise. It's enough to wake the dead.'

The vicar's wife felt a chill run down her spine.

'I'm just glad my Albert weren't here to see. Can't go wrong with a spade and a bit of hard work he used to say.'

They tutted again, their old grey teeth clicked and their hairy lips wobbled as they tottered off down the noisy High Street.

'During the war...' one began, but the noise drowned out their voices.

'Come on you lazy Irish gits,' the round man bellowed, the veins in his forehead looked as if they were going to burst. 'Put yer backs into it. Ya bunch of drink-sodden work-shy bastards.'

The huge steam-driven crane revved up its engine and let out a mighty roar as it scooped up a generous bucket of dirt and dumped it on the pavement. Almost like ants, the workmen started shovelling through it, hurling stones and rocks into one pile, soil into another.

'Keep a beady eye out for anything of any value. I heard Billy-boy found a bag of silver coins here last week, da lucky bastard. Told ol' barrel-face over there to go screw his granny... with knobs on...'

The men laughed loud and one farted. 'Better out than in I say.'

'Dat's about the most clever ting you've said all week, your arse talks more sense dan yer gob...'

Suddenly, like the angel of death, old barrel face looked up. 'Were you born lazy, or do you practise lots?' he shouted. 'I'll have you on that boat home in no time. Just because you built that bloody Titanic don't give you reason to be cocky. Now, get on with it.' His eyes wobbled in his head and the stony-faced men dug harder, remembering the years of sweat and danger from working on such a boat. When the foreman eased off, working hard, the men continued.

'Oi'll be betting dat Billy's got himself a ticket on dat ship o' dreams. The bastard's probably sunning himself right now, hangin' out wit' all the poshens, still....America eh, what a life!'

They continued their work in silence, all thinking of what it must be like on board; the drinkin', dancin' and all the pretty girls with their long auburn hair flowing as they jump from table to table, glasses full of Guinness flying through the air.

'Eye, to be sure he be having the time of his life.' All at the same time they shook their heads 'dat lucky fooken basted.'

Seamus O'Connell swung the heavy pick up in the air, expecting to feel a soft thud as it hit the loose soil. Instead it hit something so solid it bounced out of his hands and flew off across the street, narrowly missing the Vicar's wife and the grannies that had returned to stare and comment.

'B'Jesus, will you look at that now,' he said. A large round piece of wood poked from the soil. 'Must be an old tree trunk. Never hit anyting so hard in me life.'

The men scrambled around the stump, one quietly re-trieved the pick from across the road, muttering an apology to the ladies.

'Sorry girls,' he said, 'dangerous work this. When me and the lads were on the boats someone dropped a fourteen-pound hammer on me mate's head. Burst open like an orange it did. There was blood an brains everywhere.'

The ladies closed their eyes, shaking. The Vicar's wife nod-ded in sympathy for his lost comrade.

As they cleared the dirt from around the stump, Colin found another four feet away, then another next to it. The round man pushed at the small crowd that had gathered.

'Keep your heads cool lads. This is an old town; these are just trees from years ago. Probably grew here before the town was even built. Mind yer backs,' he said, as he peered closely at the stumps. They were perfectly round, solid oak and, as he brushed the tops, black charcoal stained his fingers.

'Must have burnt them down,' he thought.

With a frenzy of shovelling, the three stumps appeared close together and further digging produced a small piece of chain, about seven inches long. Colin picked it up and, as he held it, it grew so hot he had to drop it.

'B'Christ, da fookers burnt me hand.'

'Ya daft bugger,' said Seamus. As the chain hit the damp soil it hissed and sank into the dirt. Everyone watching swallowed hard.

'That is damn spooky.' said Colin. His hand was red and swelling up. The round man started pushing the crowd away, almost shooing them off.

'That will be all ladies and gents, shows over.' Clapping his hands loudly. 'Come on, come on. We're back here tomorrow. Come on, move it, move it.'

'How's the hand?' They looked at the man's large shovel-like paw. There was not a mark, just dirt from years of toil and grafting.

'It's gone, it's...'

The Vicar's wife moved swiftly home, avoiding the graveyard. In her basket she had apples for some pies, and a big bag of fresh cherries for the home-made Bakewell tarts that always went down well with the gentry. She also had some fresh cinnamon she had picked from the hollow lane next to the public house. She busied herself baking, making pastry and filling each pie with a generous portion of fruit. Her black cat purred and twisted itself around her feet, jumping on the table and meowing loudly. Reaching up to a large wooden chest, she rummaged through the collection of herbs, flavourings and small tins full of dried fruits and seeds.

'I must sort this old chest out,' she thought. 'Hoarding all this junk like some kind of old witch.'

Seamus, Colin and the road crew were glad of a short day.

'Me throat's as dry as an Arab's sandal,' he said rubbing his grubby hands around his chin. 'Be needing some of that fine ale. What d'ya calls it now?'

Colin laughed. 'One barrel of Guinness I tink, ya greedy bastad'

They slapped each other mockingly on the backs and started to wrestle.

'Children, children.' The big round man slapped them both round the heads like little boys. 'Let me get the first drinks in.'

He was, when not their boss, a good friend. He had used his influence at the boat yard when one of the men was killed and the firm did not care for his three children and young wife, left with nothing. He lobbied the local Member of Parliament for compensation for men maimed and killed at the yard, stressing that the great reputation of shipbuilders Harland and Wolff, and the 7.5 million dollars spent on the ship, was made on the hard graft and dedication of these men.

As they trudged through the slim door of the Dorset public bar, Seamus jokingly getting stuck and muttering 'Dees English, skinny runts the lot of 'em,' the pretty girl behind the bar smiled and reached for several large tankards from the shelf, her white top just hiding her ample chest.

'Now you lot, behave yourselves, this is a respectable pub and I won't be having any nonsense, d'ya hear me?'

Seamus walked up by the gap in the bar and, as the Guinness flowed like black sand, slapped her rump, which wobbled several times as she let out a loud shriek.

'You'll be keeping your grubby paws to yourself, young man,' she mocked, sticking out her tongue.

'Now dat's a fine piece of English stock,' he said, looking at his mates who were already laughing. 'You'd make any man proud to call you his lady.'

She delivered the ales and with a cheeky grin whispered into Seamus's hairy ear, 'Now don't you be telling,' she scooped out a dollop of Guinness froth and smudged it on Seamus's huge red nose 'but I ain't no lady,' to which he let out a mighty laugh and sank the pint in one, white froths also dripping down his shirt.

The round man paid for the drinks, slipping the girl some extra, a silver coin, hoping that one day she would look at him with such pretty and alluring eyes.

'Why thank you, good sire, and top of the evening to you all.'

The drinks disappeared in succession and the atmosphere glowed with warm banter and tales from home.

'I be tellen ya, dat fooken boat was big. Can you imagine... forty-six thousand tonnes?' Jaws dropped and eyes widened.

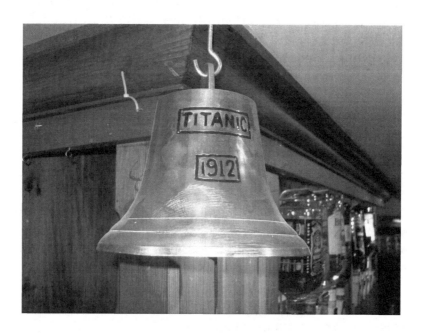

'Now you wouldn't be wanten that dropping on your foot would ya?'

There was a brief pause in the laughter as they remembered their mate.

'Still, think of ol' Billy-boy now. Probably sitting on the deck, staring at dem stars, da lucky bastad. Set sail from Southampton just recent. What be the date today, anyway?'

The round man stood up and tottered. He was one of the lads but couldn't keep up the fast drinking pace.

'Issss April fourteenth' he slurred 'hic.'

The men grabbed their glasses. 'A toast to Billy-boy.'

The pub echoed to the sound of chattering tankards, dirty laughter and Seamus could not keep his eyes off the bargirl, her full figure and dazzling eyes kept him entranced.

'Fire, fire.'

A girl from the saloon side of the pub came running at them, her face frozen in panic. 'Fire ... fire ... fire,' was all she could say.

Lauren pushed her hair away from her face. She and Seamus were staring at each other, she with her tongue in one cheek, he looking straight down her blouse.

'Where ... where ... calm down girl. Where?'

'It's in the cellar at the back bit, where all the broken chairs are.'

Lauren ran to the stairs and shouted calmly for the manager. He almost slid down the banisters. They were well prepared for any event but fire was a serious business in these old buildings. They ran to the cellar door and, pushing it open, a waft of blue smoke crept up the stairs and swirled around their feet.

In any situation or trouble in the old High Street, someone was sent to the church. There were instructions to ring the bells; three times over for fire, two for fighting and one for invasion. The bell rang three times, over and over.

Wrapping their faces in damp cloths, the manager and Lauren moved slowly down the stairs.

'The smoke appears to be coming from that door.'

There was a soft banging. It grew into loud thuds and, as the panic rose in their hearts, someone started screaming.

'It's coming from inside that room.'

It was a man's voice. He let out a low groan and then a short, sharp scream, which then turned into almost a howl.

'Jesus, there is someone in there. Hello... hello. Can you hear us?'

The screaming got louder and more intense, sending cold shivers down their spines.

'The door is jammed. The bloody door is jammed. Get all the keys,' the manager shouted. 'Every bloody one.'

Lauren dashed up the stairs to almost total peace. People were drinking quietly; even the lads were silent.

'You be alright there girl?' Seamus nodded, concern etched on his face.

'There is someone trapped in the cellar and the door's jammed. None of the keys fit ... The poor bastard will be roasted alive.'

Seamus slammed his pint on the bar and ran down the stairs. The manager was banging on the door.

'It's okay, we will get you out.'

The screaming was now getting so loud it made Seamus shudder.

'Sweet bloody Mary.'

There were two sets of screaming now.

'Oh God, there are two people in there. For fooks sake get an axe. This door is solid oak and I'm gonna have to smash me way in.'

The manager stood back as Seamus arched his back and sent the axe crashing into the lock. Blue smoke crept around their feet and they started coughing. The second scream was that of a woman. It was reaching almost fever pitch as Seamus hacked and battered the door, spluttering, cursing and, in frustration, kicking the door.

'Move you fooker' he started shouting.

As a large crack appeared, where the axe was hitting, the manager pulled his arm, moved him aside and shouted into the hole, 'Don't worry, we're here, don't panic...' to be greeted with high pitched wails and screaming so loud his head spun. Even Seamus felt fear rising in the pit of his stomach.

Colin and three other lads joined them and together they kicked, scratched and almost heaved the door off its hinges. Part of the wall crashed to the floor as the door fell with a huge thud. Through the dense smoke, which swirled around them, they searched the room. There were no flames, the screaming had stopped.

'Well, what da fook ...'

As lanterns were brought in and placed about, the smoke swished and tunnelled off through a small open window. They all looked, with mouths open, around the room full of old broken chairs and various pieces of the pub. A single piece of sandstone sat on a small table. Seamus swore five times. 'What da f...' he kept saying, 'what da f...'

At 11.40 that night, the Titanic hit the iceberg that sent Billy-boy and 1,499 other lost souls to an icy grave at the bottom of the ocean.

1668...

The blindingly intense sun broke through the lazy, fluffy clouds just as the harsh rope was slipped around his neck.

'Suppose you be wanting some sort of tip?'

It was customary for the condemned to pay the hangman to ensure a quick and easy end.

'Don't get caught,' he winked at the clumsy youth, and then he smiled. Sentenced to hang for smuggling contraband, Jack Tanner took a long, deep and possibly his last breath. Out of the corner of one eye he spotted Wilf and Robbie lurking in the tall building's shadows. He also noticed a rough wooden box on the scaffold, his next destination.

'Silly old cock,' said Wilf. 'Fancy being on the nest when the old filth came. Didn't even get to shoot his bolt. And he still had his boots on, she was well pretty an' all. You got to keep one eye open in this game, even if you are up to your nuts in guts.'

Just as Robbie started to laugh they heard the scrunching thud of Jack's neck snapping as he plunged to his end and danced like a puppet. The crowd whooped and cheered out loud, making the novice hangman smile and offer slight nods of appreciation to one and all.

As the large crowd sauntered apart, the two rascals headed to the pub for a glass or three of ale. Their throats felt jagged and raw after seeing Jack, eyes bulging and legs kicking, and eventually swaying to and fro in the cool lunchtime breeze.

'Of course, if he had a brain between his ears instead of his pants,' mocked the Dorset Arms manager, wiping the bar, 'he would have listened to me,'

Their dirty ears twitched...

'There be them tunnels all over this town. Get lost like a blind man for weeks if you don't know 'em. ...like the back of me hand I do, swear by the Lord.' His large bulbous brown eyes opened wider as if asserting knowledge and wisdom. He pursed his lips, and began to frantically polish an ale tankard: holding it up to the light to inspect his handy work.

As the ale loosened their tongues, Robbie started talking about the large consignment of French brandy, destined for nobility's tables, Wilf tried to kick his blabbering friend, only the pain from his gout-riddled foot made him yelp like a small puppy. It was due up from the coast in a few nights. The manager's eyes widened even further. Wilf briefly saw Jack's face again and shuddered. He broke Robbie's bragging and focused on old boggle-eye.

'Just supposing we do a deal.'

There was a silence and the men hunched into a tight circle. Robbie's breath and rotting teeth ensured the men re-took their own space as the manager nearly brought up his breakfast.

'Ten per cent of the profits to you,' Wilf whispered. 'No questions asked mind, and we stash the gear in these tunnels you be telling us about.'

With spit and a firm handshake, which brought the bile almost to the manager's throat, they agreed to meet at half past nine that night in the deep dark cellars of the Dorset Arms.

'Go on, ya bloody woman, push. Got more strength in one of me farts than your arms,' laughed Wilf. And on that note let out a long, squeaky, oily toot, and with his free hand wafted the obnoxious Odour in Robbie's direction.

'Now that one's got some bite to it' he snorted as Robbie's nostrils began to sting.

'Jesus, I reckon a rat has crawled up your arse and died.' Robbie quipped, his eyes watering.

The mood was happy and relaxed as the goods, dropped off from the coast with the next day's post, were rolled towards the gaping cellar doors. It took the two men all their muscle to get the barrel steady. The manager, with eyes now like thin black darting slits, pointed silently to an old oak door, which, when opened, creaked so loud that all three shuddered and Wilf saw Jack's eyes bulging. They slipped through the doorway and it groaned shut again. In the darkness Wilf fumbled for the matches and candle.

'Light the dam thing, will ya. It's like bloody hell in here.'

As the light grew, four tunnels spawned out in different directions. Take the right hand tunnel was the advice, and the men grunted like swine to get the huge barrel rolling again.

'Stop, in the name of the King,' boomed a loud voice. Robbie swallowed hard. Six armed soldiers stood in the shadows, their lanterns suddenly blinding, and pistols aimed at the shaking men's heads. It was a set-up.

'I hereby arrest you for...'

Wilf swore and had a brief vision of both he and Robbie swaying from a rope. Without thinking he pushed the barrel with all his might to confuse their captors. A pistol shot cracked out and the deafening echo throbbed around the tunnels. Robbie's head snapped back and, in the noise and smoke, Wilf saw his pal's forehead explode as the pistol ball smashed into his skull. The brandy barrel wobbled and plunged into the mild slope towards the King's men, gathering speed as they jumped

50

aside and ran towards the cellar door. Wilf took the three second advantage and scurried down the left-hand tunnel. It was pitch black and his lungs and bladder wanted to burst. In his racing mind he remembered this tunnel should lead to the church crypt, then to Escotte farm, and horses. He heard the cellar door scream open again and dull voices. His heart was pounding and he could just breathe, but in the silence he could hear the soldiers dragging Robbie's limp body away and laughing.

'He be like a pig in a poke that bloke. If he don't go mad, the rats will get him,' and the door slammed shut for the last time.

It was quiet for what seemed hours. Wilf stumbled along the slimy tunnel walls, sometimes standing, sometimes crawling. Cobwebs and dirt filled his eyes and nose, and, in the confusion, he had dropped all form of light. Cursing loud again, his ears picked up a soft thudding sound, and then it turned into a muffled banging as the soldiers started hammering large iron nails into the door, sealing it shut. His mind was empty. 'Keep moving,' he told himself. The churchyard was just across the street ... 'keep moving.'

At first, in the darkness, it sounded like running water. Then it became a faint hissing noise, like the serpent of nightmares. Looking into total darkness, a huge muffled boom filled the tunnels and a wave of dirt and rock flattened him to the tunnel floor. Rats scurried past him, over his face. Their squeaks and smells filled him with panic. Their tiny cold wet feet clambered in his eyes and hair. He closed his eyes tightly and prayed, and waited for it to end. As the rats disappeared into any small space available, he pulled himself to his knees and began crawling forward. On all fours he lunged in the dark, spitting out the dirt that filled his mouth. 'Keep moving.' In his black tomb Wilf heard the faint toll of the church bell, somewhere up in the real world of bright sun and fresh air. It rang ten times and he began to weep, 'keep moving, and keep moving.'

1993...

'Can someone change the Kronenburg?' bellowed the manager, 'they're drinking it like water.'

A staff of seven rushed, bumped and frantically clambered over each other to serve the masses of shaggy, baggy, scruffy students that filled the pub. Loud rock music crunched and battered its way around the building. The ceiling at the back end of the bar groaned with the weight of jumping, screaming, drunken people. Small pieces of plaster from the once ornate mouldings fell onto the pool table, much to the amusement of the players.

'Jesus, Health and Safety would blow a fuse if they saw this,' laughed Alf as he scurried to the cellar. 'There's going to be a few sore heads in the morning, that's for sure.'

By the side of the barrel, his eye caught a thin streak of reddish goo, oozing across the floor, and another just under his foot, causing him to slip and lose balance.

'Bollocks,' he muttered. He noticed that the trail of sticky liquid, in sparse patches, led up to the cellar steps.

'Flippin' place is falling apart.' He joked as he rushed up the stairs to the noise and smoke. Still retaining its hotel licence, the law allowed the last drink to be served when the last paying customer staggered up to bed. In other words, the staff were looking at another 2.00 am finish, even before they could have a beer themselves.

'Sod it, the Kronen...' Without thinking Alf rushed back down the stairs and, like a well-oiled machine, changed the barrel at lightning speed. Suddenly remembering the mess on the floor, and being careful not to fall arse over tit when slipping in it, he could not see a trace. Looking closer at the concrete floor, he saw a thin sooty black line. It ran from the steps to the back wall of solid brick, and stopped. He knelt down and touched it; it was dark powder, which he rubbed on his fingers and sniffed. It was so bitter his eyes filled with tears, and smelled of sulphur, which made him cough and splutter, and stung his nostrils, yeauchhh! He gasped and laughed at his own stupidity.

'Must get these old chimneys swept out. The dam soot is leaking into the cellars.'

He scampered back up the stairs. The gunpowder on the floor swished and blew into nothingness. He didn't notice the sandstone rock sitting on the stairs.

Alf, Johnny and Heather sat around the biggest table in the downstairs bar. It was 9.50 am the following morning and, after what felt like no sleep, the cleaning and restocking of the place began at 10.00. The whole pub, especially the upstairs music venue looked like a scene from a horror film. Glasses, fag butts, overflowing ash-trays, articles of clothing, broken guitar strings, way to many pairs of knickers, empty lager cans, several condoms and a neatly placed pool of sick was the standard wake up call. Some mornings they found a body or two. Nothing scary, just a couple of students so inebriated they had collapsed where they stood and crawled under a pile of coats to pass out. The toilets were another matter.

Heather had come up with the idea of drawing straws to see who gets the pleasure of donning the long rubber gloves and face mask, just so the task of removing what-ever resided in the pan was less of a stomach churning event.

54

They all sipped large mugs of steaming coffee and chomped loudly on Alf's special home-made bacon butties. The bread was crusty and about five inches thick. Heather had trouble getting one in her mouth.

'Never heard that before,' laughed Alf. It was the same old joke, but it always brought howls of hysteria to their breakfasting.

'If those students put as much energy into their studies as their drinking and dancing, this country would be on a roll,' mocked Johnny. A thick smudgy layer of tomato sauce oozed down his chin, and long streaky pieces of bacon bobbled around the corner of his mouth as he spoke.

It suddenly became very cold. Heather noticed it first and pulled on her coat.

'Is there a door open somewhere?' she said.

They all got up, leaving the food limply on the plates, and searched around the pub. The sun outside was brilliant and hurt their weary eyes as they peered, like sleepy kittens, through the curtains onto the busy High Street. Puzzled, they took their seats to resume the bacon massacre. A freezing cold icy blast swept over the table and around their feet, and Heather started to tremble, zipping up her coat as if to keep out winter. Near the cellar door she saw a shadow; it crept and crawled along the carpet.

'Look, look,' she mumbled. It was like she was on her own in the pub. Alf and Johnny stared straight ahead; almost in slow motion; almost not in the room. She squinted her eyes to look closer and could see the figure of a man, his wild hair matted in dust, mouth agape, dragging himself across the floor. She looked at his eyes; his face was barely human and, as he turned his head to look at her, his two empty black sockets stared into her soul. She felt a small trickle of pee leak down her leg as the shadow melted into the door to the cellar.

'What... what...' was all Heather could say, 'what was that?'

It seemed that hours had passed when Alf spoke.

'Flippin' hell. It's freezing in here.' The hairs on all their arms tingled and their breath gushed out of their bodies. Within seconds the coldness had gone, leaving them shaken and lost for words. Heather was the first to speak.

'Did you see that? Did you see that man?' Alf and Johnny looked at each other with their mouths open.

'No, but we certainly felt something. What the hell was that?' The once steaming coffee was stone cold; their hunger vanished. Outside the large wooden sign creaked in the soft morning breeze; the church bell rang ten times. Shaking their heads almost in disbelief, they got up to get on with the day.

'Back to work then,' said Alf cheerfully, nervously heading for the cellar. As he approached the door there were grubby finger marks, almost like scratches in the paint, and small pieces of fingernail were lying on the carpet. A shiver ran from his neck right down to the base of his spine.

'Flippin' place is falling apart,' he laughed.

1796...

Though she was only sixteen years old, Mary's parents had passed away from Tuberculosis. Her brother had joined some war somewhere and was killed on the second day and various aunts were more concerned with their day's intake of gin than her well-being.

The Dorset Arms was an impressive sight as she mooched around on the pavement outside. Pushing her nose against the large stained-glass windows, she noticed the stories that the colourful glass depicted. Three huntsmen on horses stood proud with open-mouthed and button-nosed dogs, alert and groomed. In the far corner a small fox cowered by a river, its eyes wide with exhaustion and fear. Hanging baskets swayed in the cool summer breeze and she felt warm and alive to be a part of such grandeur. She pictured herself as one of the fancy ladies, dressed in fine lace and silk. She moved her arm up to her face and gestured a graceful motion, imagining a gentle-man of quality whispering her name.

'Oi, you, Mary.' Her illusion shattered.

A short, red-faced man appeared in the doorway. In a harsh Yorkshire voice he bellowed at her. 'Get your miserable little arse in here now.'

She sauntered her cloth-covered feet towards two doors. He glared at her, bringing back memories of towering angry uncles and fear. Her eyes widened as big as saucers as she stepped inside.

'Keep moving,' he barked.

At one of the many grand, round, oak tables sat the Lords and their Ladies. A soft clatter of silver and bone china, and quiet murmurings filled the air.

'Look ahead. Don't gawp. Move it.'

Brian the manager's chest filled with pride as he pushed Mary in the back, causing her to drop her tatty bag of belongings. Pieces of silver birch twig and some shiny pebbles fell onto the soft carpet. A rabbit's foot and a lock of hair tumbled to the floor. Her two best marbles rolled off in different directions. One, in silence, meandered across the floor and, with a quiet plonk, hit a table leg. Brian's face got redder.

'You stupid, clumsy oaf,' he said and raised his hand to slap her head.

'Stop that Brian. There is no need at all.'

One of the ladies picked up the marble, looked at it, then Mary, and said 'I would like to give you a game sometime. Bet you can do smashers and grabbers.'

Mary put her stuff back in the bag.

'Bet you I can an'all, and knockees and keepses and ...'

Brian stepped in.

'I'm so sorry madam; she is just a peasant girl of no meaning. I will, of cour...'

Lady Sackville ignored him and looked directly into Mary's eyes.

'You new here then?'

Mary felt a bit giddy as, what seemed the whole world was looking.

'Yes, I be from down town way, and I...'

Brian almost had a fit and was about to grab her when the lady turned and glared at him.

'That will be all, sire, do you not have some important and deeply meaningful task to perform in another part of the building?

She was not normally that rude to people, but recognised Marys sensitive and naïve position: not unlike herself as a girl growing up in a strict male dominated and cruel chauvinist environment.

Brian sloped off, fuming.

'Hold out your hand, errm?'

'Mary,' she said, 'Mary Sumner.'

'Well, Miss Sumner, if you would be so kind as to lend me your hand.'

Mary put her right arm out. The lady's long and slender fingers moved to her blackened nails.

'If I'm going to play the East Grinstead marble champion supreme, then it must be a tidy wager.'

She placed a warm coin in the middle of Mary's tiny palm and closed her hand, cupping it and squeezing it gently. Then she smiled a smile of such warmth that Mary had never seen.

'Be lucky... and try not to fret over old grumpy guts over there.' Brian was almost hiding by the curtains. 'He is like, what you might say, a sour-faced old dog, and his bark is worse than his bite.'

Mary felt very confident and alive. She put her hand to her face and whispered in the lady's ear, 'if my brother were alive right now, he would kick his fat bum around the farmyard.'

They both laughed out loud and Mary's head was reeling with pleasure, wishing she had a family to tell of her new and elegant mate.

'Now be off with you,' the lady said in a stern manner, pointing to the back doors and winking her eye.

Mary pretended to curtsey, 'yes m'lady,' and winked back, then pulled a face like a bloated pig, nodding at Brian. She scuttled off with her face beaming and reached out onto one of the tables where a large bowl of cherries sat. Picking one up she tossed it in the air and caught it in her mouth.

A solemn and moody Brian showed her to her room; it was at the top of the stable block. She raced up the small creaky stairs.

Above the stable block was the servants quarters, and a long corridor connected it to the Hotel. Scores of small rooms, almost cell like were where all the laundry was done. There was a pressing room, an ironing room and racks of crisp white sheets and pillow cases, with the Dorset Family crest selectively sown in Gold and burgundy cotton on the corners. Four rooms were special drying rooms. These were the cats' favourites, and they were often found curled up and snoozing on rainy days.

'No mess, no noise and no fellas in here, alright' and he slammed the door and stomped down the stairs. She heard him shouting at the stable lads,

'Put ya backs into it you useless bunch of pigshits, horse-whipped in my day ya were, Get on with it' and he kicked a nearby chicken so hard it flew off down into the garden area and landed with an indignant squawk 'Horsewhipped I say'.

In her room there was a dusty window with a ledge and she climbed on a chair and pulled herself onto it. She rubbed the dirty glass with her sleeve and gasped at the view. She could see right up onto the great deer park of Ashdown Forest. She open the rusty latch and the window gave a slight creak, The houses she could just see looked like toy houses, some with long smoke trials swirling gently out of the chimneys. On a ledge near the window was a head shaped piece of sandstone, it looked like someone had began to carve the beginnings of a face, the thin lips almost smiling. It had started to get nippy so she shut the window and jumped down on the bed, one of the legs snapped clean away and she fell, half wrapped up in the covers onto the floor and laughed. She climbed back into the old wooden bed and snuggled up tight, kicking her feet together and giggling, wondering what the future held.

And so began the laborious task of cleaning, ironing and keeping the hotel and its noble guest's content. Six days a week, Mary toiled, sometimes twelve hours a day, to retire to her small attic room above the stables, keeping a diary in her own style of pictures and drawings. On the front of her note pad she drew a fat pig with wonky eyes. It always made her smile at the end of the day. The stories she heard about the upper classes, the gossip and often the scandal she dismissed as just sad people with nothing better to talk about. She was always the first to check the weekly schedule, looking feverishly for the lady's name. Her face beamed when the familiar red and blue coach clattered down the entrance to the stables, because, more often than not, Lady Sackville had a small present for her. Last week it was a large purple marble. It looked like an eye from one of the deer that roamed the forest, and she kept it in a special place wrapped in a soft leather pouch, and studied it at night in the flickering candlelight.

Even though the manager was a cold, harsh and bitter man and treated Mary like a piece of dirt, he was always rushing about, issuing apologies for the incompetence of the staff, blaming everyone else but himself. At least it meant he was not always around. The coin that Lady Sackville had given her, he had snatched away.

'Like's of you won't be needing that,' he snarled.

She didn't even know its value, but it hurt her that such kindness could match such cruelty. The coin was solid silver and Brian had stashed it away with other belongings of the staff up in his dwellings above the public house. There were rumours that he kept a wife up there; founded on the sound of vicious beatings and a woman's voice screaming out in the night, begging for mercy. A shadow was sometimes seen lurking on the stairs, almost frightened to go any further.

Mary was a very pretty girl, tall and slender with beautiful green eyes and long auburn hair that spent most of its time scrunched up in a sticky bob. But on her precious day off it flowed like a horse's mane, complementing her smooth silken white skin; a fact not unnoticed by the laughing and often leery stable lads. She felt at home, and at ease ... then it happened.

All she felt was pain. The smell of stale sweat and horse dung filled her nose. Punching her hard in the face one lad yelled, 'go on Tommy, do her good and proper.' They held her arms and legs, but no mater how hard she struggled and cursed, she was pinned to the stable floor. She cried for two days after. Standing trembling in front of the short, foul-breathed manager, she sniffed and wiped the dirt from her tear-stained face. She started to explain her ordeal, to be greeted with howls of laughter.

'Never heard such poppycock,' Brian snapped. 'You better buck up our ideas young lady or it's the workhouse for you.'

She had heard tales of vicious beatings and sadistic nuns dressed in black robes like witches. The workhouse was just down the road, a huge prison-looking building with iron bars on the windows. They say people who went in that door only came out in a cheap wooden box or chopped and diced up as dog food for the local hunt.

'Now be off with ya.'

He raised his hand as if to strike her, so she moved quickly out the door. She walked slowly down to her room. As she passed the stables the lads all stood and leered, clucking their skinny arms.

'Oh please sire, the nasty boys pulled my hair,' laughed one.

'Asking for it, anyway,' said another.

Their laughs echoed round in her head. She ran up the stairs and buried her head in the small pillow on her bed. The Lady had gone away for two months and how she needed her soothing voice and kind face. No-one spoke to her, avoiding her at every turn. An occasional whisper and giggle in her direction made her stomach churn.

As the weeks turned into months, and her unborn baby kicked her insides, the world that was so warm and bright became dark and full of nightmares. Her work suffered and, with great pleasure, Brian summoned her to his damp office.

'Well, young lady, that's it, get your stuff.' He was smiling right at her. 'Be at the workhouse tomorrow, 10.00 am sharp. No wages and no references for you, making up such tales. Mary touched the rising bump under her scruffy clothes.

'Move it,' he said, scratching his neck casually.

Back in her room she thought of her first days here, the kindness of the guests, Brian the pig being made a fool off by the Lady, her first pay-packet…But in her mind there was no future…

Placing her precious marbles in her bag, and a lock of hair from the lady, she dug deep into it, and found a small silver cross her parents had given her as a child. It was made of quite a crude metal and one edge had a sharp jagged feel to it. She

felt no pain as it tore across her arm. There was too much pain in her heart. She died at 9.56 that night, hunched in a small ball in the corner of her room, weeping uncontrollably.

They found her the next day and she was quietly buried at the bottom of the Dorset garden, in a pauper's grave at 10.00am. Brian tossed her bag into the rough hole onto her body.

'Easy come, easy go' he said and wandered of to find someone else to bully.

The purple marble fell out of the bag, rolled down her side, and landed in her hand. No one else came; it was as if she never existed.

On the Lady's return months later, she enquired as to the whereabouts of Mary and how she had missed her bubbly presence, and the games of marbles. Brian sneered.

'Well, my Lady,' he said in his best grovelling voice,

'She was not fit to work here any more, and serve the likes such as yourself.

More Earl Grey tea, madam?'

1996...

'Oh, for God's sake woman, don't you ever put anything away?' Andrew cast his eyes around the flat. It was like a bomb had hit it; a gorgeous, sexy, crazy, wild, female bomb. He could not see the carpet for skirts, shoes, stocking and various items of underwear, no doubt cast off in some great hurry. A lone boot here, a takeaway wrapper there. In fact most of the clothes she had that she wasn't wearing. He smiled and started to clear up, shaking his head and muttering, 'crazy woman. Fun ... but crazy.' The cats watched him with bemused expressions on their faces.

He and Elizabeth had moved into the flat above the old stables, which was filled with broken chairs and various pieces of the pub. In the bathroom was a kitchen sink; in the kitchen was a piece of the bath and two old beer barrels. They had worked hard to make it a home and a few calls here had given them a tatty sofa; a few calls there, some large pieces of quality carpet that gave the place an ambience. With the original fireplace open and roaring on winter nights, the cats curled up and purring, it was a warm and safe haven. He loved her so much, and wanted to care and protect her for the rest of his life: even if she was the most untidy woman on the planet.

On a warm and sunny afternoon they had climbed out of the small door in the manager's flat and clambered up onto the top of the roof, it was really high but part of it was flat, which made Beth feel a lot safer.

Andrew had brought some grub for a picnic and a half bottle of champagne, which they drank out of tatty chipped mugs and chomped on cheese and fresh bread.

'Look at the forest' said Beth 'and the chimneys, can you see the smoke trails, the houses look like toy ones don't they? And she let out a loud burp. The warm, hazy summer sun and light breeze made the green and sumptuous oak, beech and hazel trees look proud and majestic, if somewhat dwarfed. And she quite literally felt on the top of the world.

After almost two years of being there, the news came that the Dorset was to re-open, having been closed and boarded up, vandalised, set on fire three times, and practically every window smashed and smeared with childish slogans.

'Thanks for tidying up the flat,' he said. All her shoes were in neat rows, her skirts folded; even the large wooden bed had been made. Every piece of kitchenware sparkled.

'Well, I did do a bit yesterday' then she thought for a minute. She had spent most of the day in bed nursing a large hangover after dancing for nearly four hours the previous night in the car park, semi-naked. Andrew was on the pub roof shooting pigeons and repairing vandalised tiles, cursing loudly when his hand squiggled into a huge pile of crap as his head throbbed from last night's lager session.

Later that night, curled up in the big, noisy, wooden bed, a pillow fight began. The cats came flying into the room to see what the noise was.

'Well, your socks should be burned, they make me choke.'

'Well, if you didn't leave everything in one big heap.' He replied, receiving a hefty thwack around the chin, 'we might actually get to see what colour the carpet is.'

The cats, called Chicken and Teabone, just to confuse the vet, scampered into the next room, and then their little heads slid around the door again.

'Well.' The pillow caught her around the cheek with a soft plop. 'The next time you leave a huge boomer of a turd in the bog, I'm gonna scoop it out and put it in your boots.'

'Well...' thwack 'the next time I can't see out the windows for you're...' thwack, thwack, '... knickers hanging up to dry, I'm gonna put them all on my head and go to the shops...' thwack.

They started to push each other around the big bed, which suddenly lurched to the right. One of the legs had snapped clean away, and they fell in a heap on the floor, laughing. Their usual pattern of lovemaking, gentle, lingering and passionate became frenzied. He looked into her eyes, which sparkled like emeralds as she lunged at him. Her pretty mouth almost a snarl. Her white teeth clenched. Pulling his hair and scratching his back she hissed obscenities as they crashed around the room. In response he thrust harder and deeper, pushing her across the broken bed like a rag doll. Their hair was now matted together with sweat, and he mustered one final burst of thrusts which sent them both over the edge: shouting each others names whilst straining for breath. As they lay sweating and panting afterwards, the cats were at the foot of the bed, their heads at a slight angle. All their eyes met and they fell into laughter.

'Seems a bit pervy doing it in front of the cats,' she shrieked, and they both collapsed in a heap and fell asleep in each other's arms.

As if in a deep dream, Andrew's eyes shot open. All the lights in the flat were on, the water heater, controlled by a switch near the sink was flickering red. The light from the lamp in his office cast long, irregular shadows along the corridor. He distinctly remembered the bulb had blown two days ago, and hadn't yet replaced it. He heard the cat's outside screeching at the foxes and badgers, then vast amounts of scurrying. Then total silence. He got up slowly; slipping carefully from Beth's still moist warm skin, her musky scent stirring his groin once again. He gently moved her arm to her side, and pulled the cover up around her chin: her button nose twitched and she made a soft meowing sound and sniffed. He walked over to look out of the window at the pub. All the lights on the ground floor were also on. He was the only person with keys, and, besides, there was no electricity in the pub because someone had stolen the meter.

He looked around the flat. He could see the carpet. The place was spotless. Pulling on his boots, and checking for any unseen boomers, he walked down the stairs to the back entrance, when the lights flickered and it became black again. He looked back at the flat, and light from the windows lit up the car park, giving the tall trees a menacing and apocalyptic appearance. Shivering, because what he'd picked up to wear was one of Beth's flimsy tops, he hurried back.

'Be just my luck for a security guard to see me in a girly top and big boots.' He laughed.

Elizabeth was sleeping on her front, her auburn hair tangled around her face, her cute nose still twitching. She looked so peaceful and innocent, almost angelic. As he turned off the heater and the lights, he noticed the cats' food bowls were full, uneaten. He looked around the flat. Beth's clothes had been laid out in a uniform fashion, her shoes all in line by the door. In fact, every piece of her clothing was folded and placed in neat piles. His usually untidy desk was set out, pens in their boxes, papers neatly stacked. A handful of coins which he remembered chucking onto the desk were laid out in their worth order, the silver ones placed in a small flower shape. He went to turn off the lamp and as he approached the desk, it flickered and gave a slight popping sound, then went black. As he was staring at the bulb intensely as soon as the light source vanished his vision became grey and white, like a negative. He thought that someone down the road must have a radio on, at this time of night?

Because he could hear a very muffled but quite distinctive sound of a young woman singing, almost humming a simple and repetitive song: as he left the room the singing stopped. The kitchen sink gleamed and every cup was on its hook, several still moving from side to side. Usually knives and forks, pots and pans lay about the kitchen area: he opened a draw quietly and they were all in their respective slots, gleaming. The intense silver sheen hurting his weary eyes. The pots were in a lower cupboard, next to what appeared to be and old piece of sandstone: shaped like a head. Turning off the main light, he slipped back between the sheets and held Beth tight. She sniffed loudly and snuggled up to him, almost purring like one of the cats.

'That was bloody weird,' he thought, 'it's like someone else was clearing up the place.'

As her warmth and scent soothed his confusion, he respectively resisted resting his rapidly growing hard-on from prodding her in the back all night, and the lights in the pub came on again. The lamp in the office clicked and filled the room with light, but he didn't notice the cats in the corridor, staring intensely through the door at the office chair and gently purring. Like they were watching someone working.

As the Dorset began to take shape, basically everything had to go. The mass of soggy carpets, soaked with years of muddy trainers, beer and ash, were ripped out. One of the flat roofs was so thick with pigeon muck, the workmen almost chundered as they shovelled it into strong bin bags and dropped it into a large skip below. Being the only key-holders, Andrew and Elizabeth had to open the pub up at seven in the morning, and shut up at about ten in the evening. As the bells rang out, they retired to their cosy nest, which was always spotless. They both worked long hours, and thanked each other for tidying up, even though they were not at home. The cats disappeared for days, sometimes weeks, only to return with scratches and cuts and a vacant look in their eyes.

They were offered the job of assistant managers when the doors opened in the autumn of 1996. Their relationship, once based on friendship, trust and fun, became a strain and the long hours and stress saw them drift apart. She was spending more time away, at parties or clubbing in London. Her two new best pals had very wealthy boyfriends, albeit their Daddies money, who thought nothing of spending hundreds of pounds on sumptuous gifts or trips to Paris for dinner. They drove large flash cars and Beth began to wonder why she was living in a shit-hole, with two mangy cats and a poor boyfriend. She began to nag, constantly, nothing was good enough. As the pub was nearing is first day of opening Andrew had some time off and as other jobs were lined up, and after several long days had brought some fish and chips. As he climbed the stable flat stairs Beth was in the living room, it was cold because the fire had gone out. But she was dressed to kill, her perfume filled the room.

'I'm going to London, all night, don't wait up' she arrogantly scoffed and tottered down the stairs, climbing into a waiting car full of loud drunk shouty people. The car tyres squealed up the coach passage and roared off down the high street.

He threw the chips in the bin, got out three plates and cut the fish into three equal portions, removing the batter.

'One for you, and one for you, and one for me' he said as the cats came rushing over. They all enjoyed the feast, and after he re-built the fire the cats jumped on his lap, stretched out and started purring their heads off. He just stared into space, wondering what to do.

Two days later, after one nasty argument she spat out that she was better than this existence, and why didn't we have more money... forgetting she only worked part-time and relied on her rich friends for entertainment. After a long heated argument, Beth said she was pregnant, even though they took precautions, and the pressure became too much. They didn't speak for weeks and it all fell apart.

The babies were never born; they would have been twins.

When the taxi arrived at 9.56 the following morning, heavy dull rain cascaded off the roofs. The pub lights were all on and people were milling about inside, sipping mugs of coffee and marvelling at the transformation of the place. She put her three black bags of belongings into the taxi and climbed in. His lips and heart shook. The taxi sped up the coach passage and she never looked back, not even to see the tears burning his eyes. All the fun and adventures they had had at this place kept running through his mind, the laughter, the tears, the cats as kittens, pooing everywhere. Getting really stoned on grass and laying back in the car park on blankets… just watching the stars in silence, holding hands. Holding their first dinner party and incinerating a roast chicken, and having to order an Indian meal from across the road instead. Just watching her dress in the morning, and combing her long auburn hair. The smell of her perfume. Her laughter. Finding her one night in the bath, very drunk and cuddling a plastic road cone. He started to cry. He felt his heart break into a thousand pieces and, sitting upstairs alone on the sofa, stroking the cats, the bells started to chime.

It was 10.00 am.

1814...

It was like taking sweets from a blind child.

It was that easy.

Create a small diversion, look deeply worried and concerned for those affected and administer warming smiles all round.

Samuel Jackson was from moderate stock; his family owned four substantial houses in the town and he had no job description other than being a 'floater'.

'He who skives off the hard work, honesty and wealth of others' was the more common term used by folk. The stable lads just called him the 'turd', and said he was about as much use as a pipe tray on a galloping horse.

He was supposed to be living in a new brick-built villa just off the Portlands, aptly named Portland road. Instead he rented the house out for an exorbitant fee, payable in cash every month. Then, he lived it up in one of the most expensive rooms at the Dorset Arms hotel, which had been greatly improved, as next door in 1799, an elegant and grand Georgian style extension had been constructed.

The set up was easy; many of the noble guests at the hotel descended from royalty, and lived in a world of their own. The harsh reality of daily life and survival was not their concern. Making money, talking about money, and spending money was their occupation, and main hobby.

Jackson knew this all too well and his new system of thievery greatly increased his income. Bragging and bullshit were second nature to him, and the half-tipsy and gullible guests laughed heartily at his tales of hard work and keeping 'those scruffy peasants in line'.

'Well quite simply, without us,' he mocked as a pretty serving wench walked past, 'these imbeciles would still be living in caves, and dressed in rags.'

'And are they grateful? Tish and piffle, some of them can barely speak the Queen's English.'

He tittered and looked around at the pleasing glances from the guests, and caught sight of himself in the big gold leaf mirror on the wall.

The serving girl walked away, fully aware of the poison in his statements and, reaching the kitchen area, slammed the silver tray onto the wooden bench.

'That bloke, horsepoo face, whatever his name is. He either needs a good kicking or taking down a peg or two.'

She was really angry.

'Calm down Libby, he's not worth the hassle. Clowns like him seem to think they own the town and prance about in their silly garments. Us simple folk know better anyway,' reassured Katy.

'He just really gets on my tits,' she said, and realising the implications of her words the three girls in the kitchen area looked at each other.

74

'Eeeeeuuuuuuuaaaccchh,' they all said together and cracked up laughing.

'Can you imagine his slimy fingers, dog's breath and big fatty beer belly, wobbling away as he gives you the eye?'

'Eeeeeeeeeewwww'

'Can you imagine his tiny little pecker, just like one of them stringy pork chipolatas we serve up?'

She stuck her middle finger in one of the roasting pans, scooping out a big white dollop of fat and wiggled it in Rosie's face.

'Yeeeeuuuuuuchhhh.' They all screeched and fell about laughing.

'He may like to think he's the bee's knees, but it's no wonder he has to pay a girl for her services, she wouldn't do it otherwise.'

The manager walked through the doors, and said, 'Now then, less gossip and more working, you sound like a load of cackling old witches.'

He smiled at them; knowing that under their clean, starched and very uncomfortable uniforms and neatly pinned hair, there were hearts of pure gold.

'Thing is, see, the real Aristocracy were born to money, it's in their blood. Blue as your sparkling eyes,' he nodded at Katy. She was the oldest of the three kitchen girls, and the wisest. And now had the reddest face.

He treated the girls like family, seeing as his wife and had passed away in childbirth, and the future years ahead looked bleak as old age and illness, and a broken heart, beckoned.

'And with blue blood there is respect, for they appreciate hard work and decency.'

The girls stood in silence and listened to the old man's words.

'Some of the most decent and noble people I've had the pleasure to work for have been some of the most down to earth and kind, thoughtful people I have ever met'

'And, as we offer a service second to none, we get the respect and they get to wine and dine in one of this country's best hotels.'

He presided for a moment, 'and as for that jumped up parasite.' He looked through the serving hatch at Jackson, who was spinning yarns and tales about his own greatness and wealth, while continually looking in the mirror.

'He'll have a great fall someday, and you can be betting we'll be there watching.'

'Oh, an' girls, I must also inform you to report to Mr Jackson's bedchamber at 10.00pm. He has paid cash to service the lot of ya, in one sitting.'

The manager wanted to grin like a Cheshire cat and tried to keep a straight face as the look of total horror and disgust on the girls faces slowly turned to smiles.

'Eeeeeeeeeuuuuuuuuuuccccchhhhhhh,' they all squealed together and dissolved in a fit of the giggles.

Jackson's new system, as he called it, was to get the high-brow guests a bit worse for wear on vintage port, and unbeknown to them, with a small sharp knife cut their bulging and stuffed purse strings as they fell about laughing. He had done it five times now over five evenings, and no-one was the wiser. Tonight was the big one, and as he sat down to dine with the landed gentry, thoughts of vast profit filled his evil mind.

On the sumptuous oak table a porcelain vase was filled with red and yellow roses. He picked a red one out, and handed it gracefully to one of the satin-attired ladies.

'Some more Quinta de Roriz maybe? Its robust character and fruity expressions cast almost the same beauty and splendour as Madame.'

Katy peered through the hatch and caught Jackson's grovelling, 'Burrrrr...' she shivered, and mooched back into the kitchen.

'If I was a bloke I'd knock his block off.... Scumbag,' she muttered. Then she remembered his sly eye movements, and hid herself by the salt and pepper pots, peeking over them, nose first, through the hatch.

Jackson, a smarmy grin covering his face, slipped his arm just under the table, grabbed the lady's purse and quickly cut the string, and in a split second had stuffed it into his own pocket.

'No, really Madame, one should try the vintage port and maybe a cheeky little selection of cheeses.'

He clapped his hands together loudly, to create the diversion, expecting a girl to come running within seconds.

'Eventually,' he uttered.

'Another delightful creation from the superlative fromagerie of Henri de Roselle, an oral experience of great magnitude.' The table erupted into polite and dignified merriment.

'Oh really Lady De'jorrne, where did you find such a gentleman? He makes my knees quiver, and my faint heart beat almost like a drum.'

Katy slipped into the kitchen thinking out loud,

'He makes me want to throw up.'

She brought out the cheese board and Jackson immediately shoed her away. She almost ran back to the kitchen. Nearly tripping over one of the cats.

'Where's the manager, quickly, where did he go?'

'Down the cellar I think, old pooface wants more port.' Said Libby, scrubbing the skins off a massive pan of earth covered potatoes, fresh from the garden.

Rosie was peeling a huge vat of onions, tears poring down her face as she occasionally wiped long trails of snot across her arm, sniffing loudly.

Katy waited patiently; it took the poor old manager ten minutes to get from one end of the building to the other. When he came through the doors, nearly tripping over the other cat, laden with bottles she pulled him aside.

'He's up to something, that Jackson fella, swiping their purses from under their noses, I saw him do it...honest I did.'

The manager trusted Katy implicitly.

'Right, keep calm; we've got the bastard by the goolies.'

Both the younger girls sniggered as the manager clenched a mock bollock-grabbing motion with his hand. He straightened his uniform; Katy brushed his topcoat with her fingers, whilst Libby licked her hand and flattened his hair. Rosie offered to help, but with the overwhelming smell of onions on her hands the manager declined politely.

'They might think I'm French,' he laughed.

He gently cleared his throat and walked slowly and dignified towards the diners.

'My Lords, Ladies and gentlemen, please forgive the intrusion.'

Jackson looked up, annoyed.

'It appears we have a thief operating in the hotel. Please ensure your belongings and valuables are protected. If you feel the need we have a large safe in the cellar, where you can deposit your belongings overnight if need be.'

As the table erupted to gasps and mutterings Lady De'jorrne shrieked out loud.

'My purse, my purse, it's gone...oh my God, it's gone.'

'Mine too; it's been cut from my belt. What's occurring?'

There was chaos as the dignitaries flustered about, wailing and weeping at their loss.

'Please...please everybody calm down. I'm sure there is a simple solution to all this, if...'

Jackson stood up and bellowed, 'Thieving little tykes, that's them,' and pointed to Katy and the other girls who came rushing out of the kitchen amid the noise and chaos.

'Thieving little grubby tykes, always up to no good, search them now.' Jackson's face was turning bright red.

'Hear hear,' one of the Ladies spoke, dabbing her tear-stained face with some lavender-soaked hankies.

'Right, let's have some order here,' the manager almost shouted. 'My girls are not guilty of this. Sit down Mr Jackson, and would you be so kind as to empty your rather bulging pockets?'

His eyes widened and he went on the defensive.

'Don't be ridiculous, it's your thieving little scrubbers to blame. I spend my hard-earned money in here every night and you're asking me, the cheek of it all.' He looked indignant. There was stalemate. The manager, cool as a cucumber again asked Jackson.

'Sire, please just show me your pocket contents. If you have nothing to hide, I will ensure my girls will take full responsibility and pay the penalty for this crime.'

The girls stood with knees knocking by the hatch. Rosie wanted to pee.

He was rumbled. Panicking, he pushed the table to one side, sending the contents crashing about them, and started to run towards the kitchen doors. In the total confusion Rosie had gone back to the toilet, and on seeing a mad man running directly at her, picked up the heaviest saucepan from the stove. As Jackson came flying through the doors, with all her strength she swung the pan at Jackson's head. He was looking back at the restaurant so didn't see as it crashed against his skull, with a loud Kerr-pang sound. He fell flat on the floor. As he did so, coins and bank notes were sent flying from his pockets in all directions.

'Oh bravo young lady,' one of the Ladies called.

'Jolly fine show,' said one the Gents. Rosie's bladder gave way.

The local night watchman was summoned and, as Jackson groggily awoke, he was placed in a straight jacket and put under armed guard in the cellar. Just on a shelf above him was an old piece of sandstone, Right next to the bottles of port and boxes of cheeses.

At 10.00 am the next day he was taken just down the road to 'The old lock up', at the southern end of the High Street. After two weeks he was sentenced to hang at the nearby Judges

Terrace courthouse, but in a strange act of humanity it was commuted to deportation to the Australian colonies.

As they took him back to the old lock up surrounded by guards they passed the Dorset Arms.

'Oi oi, Girls…girls, look come see.'

The Manager wrenched open two of the first floor windows and the girls all stuck their upper bodies out.

'Way hay… Jacko, so you're not swinging in the breeze this morn' then?'

Katy put her hands around Rosie's neck and pretended to throttle her, and then burst into laughter.

Libby felt she could go one better, and grinned as she slipped her hand under her skirt, and pulled off her underwear, then winking at the girls, tossed her garment into the air.

A small crowd had gathered to watch the spectacle and heads turned as the flimsy pants floated in the cool summer breeze, and landed directly on Jackson's head.

'One – nil,' she yelled.

The girls laughed and punched the air.

'Oh jolly good shot,' said one of the Ladies who was standing by the main door, and shouted up, 'Bravo young woman, Bravo.'

Then the girls, who had now climbed out onto the porch, Libby being careful to protect her modesty, sat in line amongst the flower pots. Then, all at the same time they stuck out their right hands, looked at Jackson, who was peering up with one eye from the pants, and gestured a fist-clenching ball-breaking movement.

And then nearly fell off the porch from laughing.

1991...

'Well that's it, what can we do, give it away?'

The manager was standing and wiping the bar. The customers consisted of three grannies, sharing one bowl of iced cream and a rather mingy dog called 'Jeffrey ', which every now and then had a small fit, and farted... As it did so its tired old eyes rose up, looked around then went back to sleep.

There was a dirty tramp propping up the other end of the bar, saliva trails on his chest and all over the pint of cider which he hugged like a man possessed with his grubby hand. The other was in his pocket, fumbling about.

And lurking by the fruit machine was a spotty, shaven-headed fun-loving criminal. His gormless appearance accelerated by his ill fitting cloths and what appeared to be large pieces of gold toilet chain dangling from various parts of his body. His bright red cap was worn back to front, giving the overall impression of a person who wasn't exactly the sharpest tool in the box. Pumping coins into the slot and shouting in a fake south London accent 'wicked man, its wicked innit' he lost everything in minutes.

'What an incredibly sad little tosser,' thought the manager.

'I mean, do we put a sign outside saying free beer?' He sighed, 'So much potential, so much space, in the middle of town and we've taken £6.67p all day.'

He'd had to let the chef go, and four bar staff, and the crisps were so out of date he ripped open the bags to feed the birds that gathered like sinister-looking pigeon/vultures on the roof top outside. As he emptied another whole box of cheese and onion out the door he looked up.

'Might as well just start pecking at my bones, we're nearly out of food ya bastads.'

The vultures squawked and began a feeding frenzy, and the manager cursed as his foot slipped on the massive pile of muck that was building up on the flat roof outside, and was now oozing through the door.

'This town has died on its arse,' he said, at a crisis meeting at 10.00pm that night. 'We need to do something bold, something grand, and something outrageous, we need to do something, anything.'

John, the manager's mind raced frantically. He was joined by his two best mates, and three large pitchers of lager, but the ideas were running thin.

'Fancy dress, we could hold a....' spoke up Dom.

'Naaa, boring and been done to death.'

'Karaoke.' piped up Steve, 'we could have...'

'Naaa, very sad, and been flogged to death.'

'What about a rocky horror night? We could...'

'Naaa, and if you wanna dress up like a woman and prance about in suspenders, could you kindly do it at home, thank you very much.'

They all laughed, and Steve looked a bit sheepish. 'But I went out last week and got some of those frilly ones an' all, just for you mate.'

He made a mock twanging sound on his leg and they laughed even louder.

'What about naked female yogurt wrestling? I could be the judge, of course, and...'

'Interesting, put that one down as a possibility,' John laughed.

After three hours the long list they were there to brainstorm and compose had one illegible sentence on it.

'Isss a good plan,' slurred Dom.

'Isssa da dog's bollocks,' slurred Steve.

'Issssa naged flessyales yogerty bloop bloop stuff an' stuff,' slurred John, whose head hit the table where he sat, with a loud bonk.

With the bright sun, some cheery vultures cooing and a mouth tasting like the bottom of a camel cage, the morning greeted John as the alarm shrieked at 9.56am, 'Jesus, my head….'

Then the bells across the road started to clang and clatter. 'Jesus, my bloody head.'

The Bell tower was about 400ft directly opposite his bed-room, and at about the same height level.

'Must remember to switch rooms later.' He thought.

The ones at the back of the flat were a lot quieter, if you could put up with the dawn chorus of the vultures squabbling. He remembered something about yogurt, and strippers and Steve prancing about in suspenders, and shivered.

He slithered out of the bed and stuck his head in a sink full of cold water. He felt so thirsty he began to drink in great slurps from the basin, only stopping when he noticed that someone had thrown up in it the night before, and little specks of carrot and a couple of cigarette butts were floating around the oasis.

He stomach contracted and he heaved about two pints of water, in a projectile style, out of the luckily open window. It cascaded down the tiles and bobbled off down the guttering. The vultures swarmed and one silly bird flew of with a cigarette stub in its beak.

'Don't take up the habit mate, very addictive.'

As he laughed his head throbbed, but at least he felt vague-ly human again.

'Bacon butties, that's what we need,' he thought, and wandered off to the kitchen downstairs, wondering where Steve and Dom were.

As he passed through the first-floor restaurant, he heard a muffled groaning, and in one corner the large burgundy curtain had been ripped down and pushed about, in a heap. He pulled the material to one side and there was Dom, looking like death warmed up. Two big round bloodshot eyes peered from the makeshift bed.

'Uuurrrrgaaaa.'

'Hello Mate, how's the head?'

'Uuurrrrgh. Water, bacon butties and water...now. And Christ I need a piss. What's with the bloody bells man? This place is so weird, I can feel the bones in me head rattling, and so many weird dreams, and I could hear a baby crying, what's that all about?'

'That will be the lager mate. Mouth like a camel cage?'

'Yup.'

'Me too.'

Steve was nowhere to be found.

Bacon sizzled frantically in the pan and the radio bumped out a happy groove, and they knew all the words, sadly.

'Naaa, sod Abba, burn all the hippies, what we need is some good loud rock music.'

Just before the 'strolling bones' blasted from the speakers, John's ears switched on. There was a loud banging and crashing noise coming from one of the south side rooms up in the top flat. And giggling, lots of it.

As the breakfast burnt to a cinder John and Dom walked, not too quickly, up the stairs and headed to the source of the noise.

On a large double bed in the stack room, so called because most of the room was filled with one of the main chimney stacks, there was a mass of arms, legs, feet and hair, and even more giggling. All tangled up in the duvet was Steve, and his head peered over the cover, grinning.

'Errm. Morning chaps, errmm... I got a bit side-tracked last night. You passed out, and you fell over in the bogs, lightweights.'

As he spoke two girls emerged either side of him, nudging under his arms and yawning.

'Where the bloody hell did you find them?' Dom asked open-mouthed.

'Oi, Cheeky, do you mind.' The girls winked and yawned even wider.

'Ha ha, they saw the lights on and came in the back doors last night, which Jonathan; I hasten to add, were not locked.'

John looked at the floor, 'Well you know...'

'Any Tom, Dick or Harry could have walked in. Luckily for you and for me,' he rolled his eyes and dropped his jaw, 'we have Debbie and Shelly here to thank. And I'm sure the manager and his team here at the Dorset Arms would like to show their gratitude by...' he paused, dropping his jaw again, 'by getting on with the bacon butties and sorting coffee out. As soon as possible. I thank you...'

He nodded at John, who stood like a zombie, as the hangovers clouded their judgement. That and the fact that Debbie's smooth legs and naked body were just visible under the duvet.

'Bacon,' Dom shouted, and ran down the flat's stairs at full speed to the smoky kitchen. The bacon had shrivelled to thin black crisps, and he muttered and tipped the lot into the metal bin.

'Incinerated pig anyone?' He shouted up the stairs loudly to be greeted by an even louder, 'boo, rubbish,' mainly from the girls.

'So it's toast all round then. Well, at least I didn't burn the coffee.' He shouted up again.

The coffeepot was about 2cm short of empty and hissing loudly, just about to explode.

John reluctantly wandered off, but just couldn't resist,

'At least we didn't find a bloody piglet,' and burst into hysterics.

'Shut it,' said Steve, 'you promised.' Then disappeared under the covers to hide his embarrassment. The girls looked puzzled at the joke, and then joined him, giggling.

As the lads got one of the big round tables ready in the restaurant, they heard the thundering sound of the girls running up and down the top corridors to jump in the bath. Then running back several more times and shrieking loudly, then more giggling and splashing.

'Oh, to be a fly on the wall of that bathroom,' sighed John.

'Oh, to be the soap.' Dom added.

Steve walked in, in just his pants, scratching.

'Mate, put it away, we're about to eat.'

As they sat down, with two places set for the girls, and waited for more bacon to cook, Dom nudged Steve in the ribs,

'So mate, what was it like? You know, wink wink and all that.'

'I don't know what you mean.'

'You know, two girls, one big bed and...'

'Yeah yeah, that's for me and the walls to think about, wink wink.'

'Bastad.'

'I will say one word.'

The lads sat open mouthed.

'What...What...?' they urged.

'Loverrrllly....ha ha. There is something about that room though, it just makes you feel so horny, and it's quite odd.' He smiled deeply. 'Oh, and just that little added treat of a couple of naked, totally up for it women.'

'Bastad,' they both said together.

As the girls came in, smelling like fresh roses and all shiny-faced, the feast began. Loud chomping and slurping ensued and the table ate in silence as sustenance was definitely on the menu.

Shelly spoke with a mouthful of bread and bacon,

'So what were you lot up to last night then, sitting up so late and getting so hammered?'

John finished his fourth sandwich, swigged his sixth cup of coffee and sat back rubbing his belly.

'Aaaaaa, that's better. Last night. Well, me and the boys did have a plan to come up with the brilliant idea to kick this place up the arse,' he began 'but then due to circumstances beyond our control....'

'You just got pissed up... typical. Bloody typical,' said Debs.

'Well... yes, but it was fun, and we did get some ideas out, and... Wasn't that bacon well cooked this time? I can...' His words slowed up.

Steve just couldn't stop grinning, and winking at both the girls.

'Course you know what would be cool, really cool?'

They all stared across the table at Debs, whose eyes were rolling about; sussing out the potential...Her borrowed white shirt was covered with splashes of coffee and tomato sauce.

'Live music. You've got the space. Set up a bar over there.' She pointed to one corner.

'But that's Dom's corner.'

'What do you mean?'

'It's where Dom likes to pass out after a session,' John laughed, and slapped him on the back. Dom grinned and hid his face with a coffee cup.

She huffed at the lad's laddishness and continued:

'A stage area over there,' she pointed to the far corner. Turn it into a sort of special exclusive club. I might know a few people in the music business and, wagons roll.'

Her judgement was implicit.

She slapped her thigh… 'Yeeeeeeeehhaaaaarrrrr…..'

The idea sank in two days later.

An even bigger skip was ordered and the gang started the task of making a music venue. It was hard graft, and to reduce noise pollution all of the windows on the first floor were stuffed with soundproofing and boarded up.

A small but solid stage was constructed of old pallets and inch-thick hardboard. The bar came together with moderate ease as the beer, lager and cooler lines were run straight through the floor from below. The whole place was painted black; everywhere was given two coats. They found a piece of old sandstone, which became a handy door wedge.

At the end of the third night the workers stood back, con-gratulated themselves on a good job and slumped on the big round table.

'What ya gonna call the place then?' Deb said. 'How about *Debbie's Den*?'

'How about *Debbie does East Grinstead*,' laughed Shelly.

'Oi, less of that. It's just a rumour.' Debs tossed her hair back and grinned like a minx…on heat.

'It needs to be something rock and roll. Something to sum up all this hard work.' John spoke.

'What about *Hollywood nights*?'

'Crap.'

'*The Chinese knocking shop*?'

'Crap.'

The girls looked puzzled.

'Sorry girls, private joke.'

'What about *Piglet's corner*?'

'Hey, that's a good name.'

'Its total crap,' perked up Steve, scowling at John.

Thousands of pieces of paper were put in a hat, and drawn. Each idea got the same comment.

'Crap, crap, not bad, crap, crap......'

At about 10.00pm the large pitchers of lager slammed on the table, Dom had just got a momentous curry from across the road and once again the paint-splattered, bruised-thumbed and knackered crew sat around the table and scoffed. The girls had picked some wild flowers from the meadow that day and put them in an old chipped porcelain vase they had found in a cupboard in the cellar. Next to it was an old piece of sand-stone.

As the girls collected all the plates and glasses to take to the kitchen, the lads finished up with the hovering and final cable laying, PA and lighting rig instalments.

Dom quietly spoke to Steve. 'How was it, really? I mean two babes...at once?'

'Mind-blowing.' Steve blew his breath out in one big blast. 'Phewww...,' and added, 'So you're just a one-on-one kinda bloke then?'

'I should be so lucky.' Dom said with a glum expression.

'What did you just say?' John peered from under the stage with his hair stood up on end and covered in dust, as the girls came back with more pitchers of fresh lager.

'Errrm, Mind...'

'No the other expression.'

'Er...pass.' He nodded at the girls, slightly embarrassed.

'One on one, that's it...101... Brilliant...The 101 club. It's so rock and roll. It's brilliant.'

'The 101 club.' John kept saying it. 'It's bloody brilliant.'

'The 101 club. Hey I like it,' said the girls at the same time.

'How the hell did you think of that?'

'A flash of inspiration,' said Steve, thinking about the other night's shenanigans in the stack room.

Five pint glasses were hastily filled with lager, and the gang crashed them together loudly.

'To the 101 club. Get ready East Grinstead 'cos we're gonna rock this old town to its foundations.'

The opening night was planned in great detail, tickets and flyers were printed, posters slapped on every door, window and shop front. Much to the distaste of the local council, who had more than slight reservations about a live music club right in the middle of the sedate old country town.

Two councillors had driven by earlier and seen large amplifiers and huge black boxes, covered in stickers being man-handled through the main front doors... And what appeared to be scores of scruffy students and long haired denim-clad rockers loitering about, smoking those long and funny looking cigarettes.

They both tutted and shook their heads.

Debs booked the first band to play. Some mates of hers who were gigging in and around London had a week off and had agreed to do a short set for a laugh, and free drinks and somewhere to crash the night.

They were on a promotional tour of the UK, and their tour bus screeched and wobbled down the old coach passage and parked in front of the stable block. The driver let off the air horns with a mighty blast and all the vultures on the roof fluttered off in disgust.

'G'day mate,' said Libby, the singer and guitarist. 'Geez, what a spooky old place, gives me the willies.'

John, Dom and Steve grinned as the girls climbed out of the bus, their short skirts and tanned legs a fine sight on a cool summer evening.

Debs went ballistic, jumping up and down and grabbed Shelly by the arm and linked up with the three girl musicians. The gang of five strutted up the back metal stairs, yakking so intensely they barely paused for breath.

'This is gonna be wild,' said Dom.

John reached over and pretended to push up Dom's lower jaw, 'Calm down boy, we've got work to do.'

Steve's imagination went into overdrive.

The 101 club was heaving; the whole downstairs was also packed out. John had hired extra staff in anticipation, and extra booze. A second dray lorry load to be precise.

He looked nervous. There were many more people than they had ever expected. The old restaurant now resembled a full-on venue, with people from all walks of life looking around at the place in awe.

Several journalists from NME and Melody Maker had turned up, eager to see and hear this new 'girl' band with attitude, on hearing reports from the London 'B' venues. Apparently also in the crowd was a woman who worked for Island records, with pen in hand.

Libby, Katy and Rosie strutted onto the stage in semi-darkness, the atmosphere was charged with electricity and anticipation. Then a strobe light started to flash, making the girls look like an old black and white film, and they just stood...and waited.

It went pitch black again.

The huge crowd roared and within seconds the stage was ablaze with red, orange, yellow and green flashing light. Libby smashed her guitar with her fist and yelled at the top of her lungs.

'Hey 101…101…101, get a load of this. We're girls and we're loud,' and the band blasted into what John described later as 'The female Led Zeppelin on speed.'

Within seconds those at the front who hadn't had their eardrums shattered began to jump up and down, and the whole first floor erupted into party mode. Big time.

Libby and Katy were in serious performance mood, and as Rosie sat with her eyes shut and teeth clenched bashing the shit out of her drums, the two front girls were in their element.

At one point Katy had the microphone stand between her legs, rubbing her groin on the hard silver boom and thumping the bass like a mad woman.

John almost blushed. Steve was in heaven and Dom stood open- mouthed. Debs and Shelly were right at the front jumping around like wild animals.

Some of the older members of the audience at the back started to leave, disgusted by such antics. Everyone else just went crazy.

At the back of the stage a large sign swayed in the noise and racket. It read: **This is the 101**.

Just below it hung a worn and tatty banner with equally big letters. It read 'The Jackstones'.

The girls played for an hour and a half non-stop. They did one ballad, a cover version of 'Knocking on heaven's door' which the audience swayed to and sang along.

A couple of local lads, scared by the ferocious wild cats on stage started to heckle.

'Hey babe, you can knock on my door anytime, ha ha, nice tits an' all, ha ha.'

Libby kept the music going, waving her arms down so Rosie knew to quieten up. She looked at the lads who were smirking like idiots, and taking the microphone out of the stand, started to walk seductively towards them. They looked at each other nervously.

She made sure every eye was on her, and began to kiss and lick the microphone like a giant cock. Looking really mean she pounced. And encouraged the audience to start chanting, especially the female members, 'losers, losers.' Then, in her broad Australian accent, she let rip.

'Suppose you boys be wanting a fuck tonight then? Just suppose me and the girls take you little boys down the cellar laters and give ya one eh? What do yer reckon people?'

The audience went wild and started clapping and chanting.

'Just supposing me and the girls don't like snotty little English boys eh? Especially ones wearing,' she scoffed loudly, 'pink shirts. Hey…fair-dinkum fellas.' She held out her wrists, limply.

'Just to let yas know, we only fuck real men, not jumped up ponces with pappy's money in their pockets. Ya be getting the message, ya scrawny looking mungrels?'

The lads withered and slipped quickly out the doors, the deafening sound of female laughter ringing in their ears.

'Well, hey…that taught the bum faced dingoes not to piss with the Jackstones, not unless ya want ya fucken googlies ripped off, hey.'

The band started another song, really fast. The energy and adrenaline pumping was sending the audience into frenzy. Debs had to scream into Shelly's ear, hurting her throat.

'I've never seen them play so good or loud.' And carried on jumping and sweating almost to the point of collapse.

The band finished the last number, and ran off the stage, each girl in turn giving the crown a 'V' sign with their fingers.

They had arranged to stay in the stable flat that night and the five girls ran shrieking and screaming down the back stairs, across the car park and scampered up the stairs with the grace and elegance of a pack of wild dogs.

Debs and Shelly were so grateful that John had let them use the stable flat. They had had a nose-about last week and the place was full of old broken chairs and various pieces of the pub, but got a shock when they walked into the main room.

It was all made up, with cushions and pillows, soft lights and a gleaming CD player sat on a low table. On the sink was a big silver bucket, full of ice and a bottle of Moet, and bags of crisps and nuts.

Plump sandwiches sat on paper plates, and on the centre of the table was a large glass bowl full of exotic fruits.

'Geez,' said Rosie.

'Crikey,' said Katy.

'Well fuck me sideways,' said Libby.

'So tell us again about the name 'The Jackstones',' said Debs, her mouth crammed with crisps.

'Well our old gramps, that's grandpa to you guys.' Katy swigged hard on the bottle, which sent the bubbles straight up her nose. She spluttered and let out a huge belch, 'looked up our family name from years ago. It seems some bloke called Jackson, Samuel I think, was sent over from this place, East Grimstead.'

'Its Grinstead,' chipped in Shelly and belched even louder.

'Yeah whatever. Seems he was some sort of crimmy, thieving an' stuff and, rather than stretch his neck,' she let out a long 'hhuuurrrgggggga' sound and all the girls winced, 'they shipped him over to Oz. It made an honest man of him, reformed character you might say. He set up a business and we're the result, loud and proud grand-kids, kinda spooky eh?' She belched again.

The gang cackled and finished the bottle, and Libby stood up and tottered, 'Got us a crate of white wine in the wagon, hang on to ya snatches, I'll only be a jiffy.'

She was gone for about 15 minutes, and the girls were starting to worry.

'Bet the silly bitch has gone walk about, better go look. Or she's pulled one of the poncy fellas and has got a hot bell end in her gob.'

Katy laughed and the girls heaved each other up and came out the flat and started searching around the car park, looking under cars and in old outbuildings.

'Hey Libbs. What are you playing at girl? We're in serious party mode here, don' fuck it up ya drongo.'

They heard some raucous laughing coming from the front of the pub. The girls scarpered up the coach passage and a large crowd had gathered at the front doors of the building.

Then they heard Libby, at the top of her voice, shouting, swearing and laughing like a hyena. She was standing on the porch, in-between the flowerpots with her knickers in one hand and a bottle of wine in the other.

'Come on ya dickbats, which one of you lucky fellas want me grundies then? They're all good an' juicy too.'

She whooped like a wild cat and chucked the pants into the air. There was a mad scramble as most of the lads made a desperate grab for the flying garment, which spun in the air and, almost in slow motion and with a satisfying squelch, landed directly on someone's head.

Libby screamed with delight and with her hand gestured a mock ball-breaking motion.

'Hey people…One-nil,' and nearly fell off the porch from laughing.

John was in his bed, sideways, with a sink full of vomit and the window open.

Steve was in the stack room, but had waited so long had fallen asleep and was gently shagging a pillow and whispering 'Debs, oh Debs oh'

And Dom was a corner of the 101, all wrapped up in a burgundy curtain, dreaming of bacon.

1855...

It had all gone so wrong. Through the dense smoke and cries of pain, Captain Lancaster watched as over three hundred of his men took the full force of cannon head-on. He was informed that the enemy was eighty miles away and desperately low on ammunition; how could this be happening? Tired, and with a raging thirst, he rode all night away from the carnage. Images of shredded and limbless men, wandering or crawling, filled his racing mind. The dirt, sweat and blood on his hands and clothes mingled with the horse's skin; its nostrils flared out great white plumes of breath, like the ghosts of men who now lay dead in the mud.

Through great wafts of blue smoke and backslapping, the generals agreed – this was a laughing stock. The Prime Minister was appalled; the press had gone to town with cartoons of fat generals smoking cigars sitting in pushchairs and swigging from gin bottles.

'The British Army could not, and would not, tolerate such a defeat,' said one, lighting a cigar and sinking his fourth glass of Bombay sapphire. 'Someone must carry the can,' he bellowed, farting loudly.

'Hear, hear,' mumbled another, just waking up.

The Captain was summoned to Horsham in Sussex, to be charged with deserting his post, cowardly conduct and disobeying strict orders to hold the line. He desperately tried to explain the situation, but the general's just tutted and coughed.

'In my day, sire, you would have been shot on the spot. Blind coward's pardon, they called it,' and he let out a huge wheeze and started to go bright red. Unbeknown to the Captain was the fact that the red-faced general's son was coming up the ranks and some space at the top was needed.

A court-martial was set for ten o'clock the next day at East Grinstead. It meant certain death by firing squad by the hands of his own countrymen. He took the next coach and arrived at the hotel in good time. Being an officer meant he was granted one last night, and with a heavy heart, he looked up at the beaming windows and the warming interior of the Dorset Arms as the coach clattered down the passage to the stables.

The striking white full moon cast deep shadows across the garden, smoke from the chimneys danced like graceful ballerinas, swirling about the rooftops. Plump flowers of wisteria and summer jasmine hung like bunches of fruit and water droplets sparkled like a thousand moths captured by the flickering gaslight. There was a quiet murmur of horses and stable boys playing blackjack in the rooms above the stable block, and the air was filled with a warm peace. No guns, no cannons, no screaming ... just a soft, warm peace. Time stood still.

He looked down at the bowling green on the lower terrace. The grass was smooth and glistening, and two black and white cats were sitting in the middle. One was perched alert; its eyes wide as it stared into the black woods; the other gracefully, if not elegantly, began to chew the head of a limp mouse. In the distance foxes barked, their desperate cries echoing through the still night, and the badgers tumbled and fumbled amongst the bracken and scurried deeper into the dark tunnels. From the white lights of the buildings he could see carefully designed flower beds and boarders: Blue-eyed Iris, Coreopsis and Crocus Boryis were planted in neat rows. He could just make out the soft blue-purple flowers, which as night fell closed togeth-er, scrunched up as if hiding in the shadows. A large patch of Evening Primroses, their bright yellow flowers wide open, almost embraced the darkness. Scattered about were large pieces of sandstone, he stared at one: it almost looked like a face, and was smiling. Tall majestic stems of Foxglove, Delphinium and Golden rod gently swayed together, and by a small pond a mag-nificent specimen of Gunnera Manicata loomed over the clear water: It's Jurassic like spiky stems and leaves a stark contrast to the soft white water lilies below. He could hear frogs arguing. Their tiny squeaky mating calls adding to the serenity.

Ever since he could walk, he remembered charging around the paddocks at home on a wooden play horse. A pretend sword in the hand, and teeth gritted, he would gallop up to the small bail of straw, swishing at it feverishly, cursing aloud all those who stood in the way of the British Empire and greatness. His father whooping with joy as he plunged the lethal weapon into its guts, and grinning.

'One day, my son,' he bellowed, dotting his small round shiny face with specks of saliva, 'your country will be proud of you.'

Then he remembered their robust nanny, 'Nam Nams' they called her. She was of Caribbean origin, and her face always carried a warm and mischievous smile. And she was so kind. So very kind.

On Friday lunchtimes she opened the big stable kitchen doors quietly, and whistled... John's ears pricked up in delight… as she had the icing sugar bowl filled with scrummy leftovers: and with a big wooden spoon John would stuff his face, most of the sugar ended up all over his hair and shirt. But Nam Nams always made sure he was cleaned up before supper, rubbing a course towel around his head and face, much to his protests.

'Yous mama and Dadda see yous in that state boy they skin me alive, I'm a telling ya…' her big brown eyes rolled in their sockets and she let out a mighty laugh.

'Yes sir, they be woopen my behind till next Friday' Then she wrapped her huge arms around him and gently squeezed, almost taking his breath away.

There wasn't any affection in his family, and never having brothers or sisters the only real cuddles he received were from Nams, and he loved her so much for it. He felt safe and secure, warm and loved.

Lost in his thoughts John lit a cigarette, drew deeply and let the smoke blow across the quietness.

On one occasion Nams had spilt some expensive wine from the decanter, all over the starched white table cloth, and his father began ranting and raving, waving his arms about and cursing her out loud.

John never understood what his father was saying but it was something about being put back on the boat, and he wept into his pillows that night fearing Nams was going to leave.

She had heard his sniffles and gently sat on the bed.

'Don't go Nams' he pleaded.

'I's going nowhere boy' she reassured him.

Her huge brown eyes rounded wide.

He climbed out the bed, crawled up to Nams and hugged her, almost repaying the kindness she showed him on a daily basis.

'Hey, I's just a silly old woman, bit clumsy and butter-fingered, and life's to short for tears young man, sleep tight and I's be seeing yous in the morn'.

She let out a very quite but typical laugh, muffling her face with her hand. John laughed to, his face cheeks still stinging from the tears.

'Sleep tight my little soldier' she said smiling and ruffling his hair.

'Gonna be baking some mighty fine cookies in the morning, chocolate and Coconut chip ones at that'

He loved her cooking and baking skills, as his mother 'Never had the time' to do such demeaning work, and his tummy rumbled loudly as he drifted of to sleep dreaming of eating Nam's cookies with a nice glass of fresh farm milk.

In full uniform of scarlet and black jacket and trousers, with gold-braided collars and cuffs, he walked around to the front of the hotel and, straightening his back, pushing out his shoulders and removing his cap, he moved silently into the building. The warmth hit him and the sweet smell of perfume and ale filled his lungs.

The pub was quite full, people were politely chatting and sharing long complex stories, every now and then a table would erupt into a bursts of laughter:

'So I said you're meant to hold it with both hands and shake it' a tall well dressed man concluded: and made a vigorous gesture with both hands. Several of the Ladies held their napkins to their faces, trying to hide their merriment and embarrassment.

'An then he said can I do it with my feet as well' to which to whole table collapsed into deep hysterical laughter.

He had heard the joke on the front lines, although he imagined due to the nature of the guests the version told here was not of the same crudity, or indeed vulgarity as the version the soldiers told.

He walked slowly across the soft burgundy and gold carpet, nodding and smiling at the happy punters, with not a care a in the world except enjoying the warmth and banter: and another round of drinks. On one table an elegant collection of red and yellow roses, with long spikes of bulrush stems and Mares tails filled one corner. Perched neatly next to them were two Ladies of a fine distinction, and they beckoned him over.

What was he going to say to them? Could he make polite conversation? Would they understand his state of mind?

Would they care? He looked over and waved, and pointed at the bar. Just at that moment the tall well dressed man stepped in front of him, and began cracking jokes and ordering the ladies drinks: John was very relieved.

CRIMEAN WAR 1854-1855.

Breathing in deeply again, he ordered a large whisky at the bar. His hands were shaking, so he sank the first drink almost immediately, and ordered another. Downing that, he politely asked for the half-full bottle, which arrived on a silver tray with a new clean crystal tumbler. He was about to take a seat near the window, when the landlord appeared.

'Well, bless my old cottens,' he said, 'its Captain Johnny boy, back from the wars I see, and look at that, not a scratch on him.'

He felt the whole bar staring and hid the whisky bottle with his arm. Several of the bar girls looked over, their doe-eyes hazy and lids fluttering.

'So, you been hard at it, my son,' he continued, slapping John's leg.

'You know me, mate, always up for it,' he lied. The whisky had started to take its magical effect and he began to relax, almost forgetting the reason for being there.

'Not much has changed around here,' his old friend Simon, said, 'The place has had a lick of paint. They plan to dig up and replace some of the knackered High Street, probably take them years to get round to it." He laughed. 'So how are you mate? Been a long time?'

They sat on a comfy old sofa.

Simon beckoned to the bar, and one of the girls brought his drink over, a long slow gin and tonic with fresh lime segments.

He whispered to John as she walked back to the bar,

'That's Emily, fit as a butcher's dog and a real beauty' he smiled, 'one of my best girls' he chortled.

'Hummm, very nice' said John; nodding his head and admiring her shapely legs and smooth black silk stockings.

Emily could feel two sets of eyes burning into her backside and put on her sexiest walk, giggling out loud.

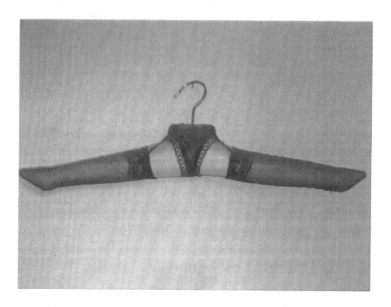

Simon had to rush off to the top floor, because some guests had complained about strange shrieking and banging noises coming from the stack room. An elderly Lord had gone missing and two of the laundry maids hadn't been seen for over an hour.

'Never a dull moment eh mate? Don't go away, won't be long... you be ok for a minute? He raced up the stairs.

John had finished the bottle and rose unsteadily to his feet. He was just staring into space. 'Fine,' he slurred, 'jusss fine.'

He bumped his way to the stairs by the front doors, turned and slowly walked up the soft red carpet. The buckles on his boots gave off a slight jingle as he took one step at a time. As he climbed to the gentlemen's rest rooms on the first floor he started to have flashbacks; he could hear the screams, the booming cannons, the crash of steel and the look on the dead men's faces, frozen in terror. He steadied himself, splashing cold water on his face. As he looked up into the large ornate mirror, his blood ran cold. No longer was there the face of a young, important, upstanding officer. What peered back was that of a coward. The word echoed inside his head. It suddenly hit him what was about to happen in the morning. The generals would be there, reeking of stale gin, as he would be led blindfolded to the corner of a field and shot like a rabid dog.

His only thoughts of consolation were that his mother had passed away years ago, and his father was in an asylum for the mentally unstable. 'The years of front-line war had caused him to lose his marbles,' they said. He laughed out loud, briefly loosing his balance and crashed into a small chest by the sink. As the door flew open there was a head-shaped piece of old sandstone sitting on a shelf, and the Times newspaper fell onto the fired-earth tiles and opened its pages. **'BRITISH ARMY SEEKS GLORY IN SUDAN'** the headline screamed. He squinted his drunken eyes. Just below was a cartoon of the generals, the fat nasty generals swilling gin with word captions issuing from their arses. In his top pocket a small bottle of arsenic awaited its release ... and his.

They found his body the next day at 9.56 am. He lay, eyes open, against the water closet, his arms clutching the white bowl and drool covering his chest. The laundry-maid screamed so loud, smelling salts were wafted under her nose for minutes. Simon, who was excluded from military service due to chronic back pain, made sure his friend was taken care of, arranging a small service at a local church. Only he and Emily attended, she did not know John but shared the deep feeling of sadness and waste as the black rooks in the treetops squawked and mist settled in a quiet piece of England. It was as if he never existed.

1992...

As Clare cheerfully shut the main front doors, bolted them tight, and drew the curtains, she felt someone staring at her from behind. As she turned, expecting to see a drunken student, with one shoe on, belching the alphabet and grinning stupidly, there was no one there. The curtains pushed out from the doors so violently it felt they were attacking her, and she put her hands to her face as if in protection. They settled quietly and she pushed the hair from her face. She looked at them, puzzled, and walked off around the pub, clapping her hands loudly so as to scare revellers from the shadows.

'Come on you morons, get out. I've just done a twelve-hour day and I'm knackered. Come on, move it, move it.' The pub was strangely quiet. A soft plop from a leaky tap caught one ear; a whirring from a fruit machine caught the other. In between, distant cars rumbled into the night.

'Silly bastards,' she muttered, laughing at talking to herself.

She hit the switch on the machine and all the lights in the pub flickered. It went pitch black just for a few seconds and a shiver ran down her spine and her throat felt tight. In the light from the outside street lamp, there was a man standing right next to her, smiling. He was wearing what looked like an old uniform, sort of military and he was quite good looking.

'Sorry about the lights, mate, and 'she said, 'bloody place is fall...'

As the lights came back on she was alone. Her heart began to beat faster and she looked around, checking behind the bar. She stood totally confused.

"But he was standing just there, wasn't he?'

There was something missing on the wall. One of the old pictures had gone. Her mind raced frantically, trying to remember which one it was.

Where, over the years the sunlight had faded the timber panelling, there was just a dark brown square where the picture had hung. She knew practically every picture off by heart as she spent an hour once a week cleaning the glass and dusting the frame. But her mind was blank.

'Was it the cheery jockey on a horse? She though as she walked around the downstairs bar, 'or the plump Chef holding a large carving knife? Both those pictures were still on the wall.

As she came around to the front doors the curtains were very gently flapping, almost in wave formation, and it became very cold.

Then it hit her. It was the charcoal drawing of Captain Lancaster that was missing. The small hairs on her arms started to tingle as she recalled how, when walking in any direction from that drawing the Captains eyes followed her around the room. The charcoal sketch captivated her and she made a special effort to make sure the glass was sparkling and frame polished. She had often noticed the drawing was damaged; there was a large rip down one side which, that had torn across the old yellow paper. The slashing nature of the cut had started at the bottom of the frame, and finished as just a small thin line, right across the Captain's neck.

She stared at the blank space.

'Maybe it was being repaired? She thought, 'although she had only cleaned it this morning!

She shivered again and collected the tills from the bar. They had to be cashed up and put in the cellar safe. The manager was away at a meeting in London and she felt proud that, at twenty-two years old, she was in charge, and lifted her head up as she walked towards the cellar door. There was that sound, a soft thud and a jingle of metal. It was coming from the stairs. She listened again ... Someone was walking slowly up to the first floor. It sounded like someone very drunk.

Just at that very moment, Rachel came crashing through the cellar door, singing and smiling. Her heart missed four beats.

'Flippen 'ell girl, was that bloody spooky or what? There I was with me knicks round me ankles, just about to park me arse on the pan, and blamm... pitch black.' She laughed.

Clare came crashing back to reality.

'Talk about if you sprinkle when you tinkle.' She gave a little demonstration with her hands. 'But I was a sweetie and wiped the seatie.' She laughed again really loudly.

Clare had forgotten she was in the cellar; her head was in another place.

'Yeah, yeah, that was kind of weird. Come on girl, get the vodka out. When the cat's away and all that. We can put on the Red Hot Chillies nice and loud.'

She started dancing and mimicking the lead singer, twisting her arms and hopping on one foot.

'Give it away now, give it away now, uuuurgh, uuuurgh.' She started singing, completely out of tune.

The two girls flopped on to one of the big comfy sofas, vodkas in hand.

'Not tonight Rach, I'm up at eight tomorrow, get the cleaning done, the bottling up, the bars sorted. Ya crafty cow, got out of that one didn't ya? Clare mimicked the look Rachel gave the manager as he left at lunchtime. 'Soppy-eyed hussy. If you had fluttered your lashes any more, your eyes would have popped out. "But I don't do mornings" ... ya tart.'

The girls sat in silence for a while, listening to the silence.

"Right then, let's have some fun with this" Rachel pulled up her big wonky handbag, scuffled about in its vast depths and pulled out an old Victorian gaming board.

"Me Nan used to play with this when she was a girl, and she taught me how to use it"

"What the hell is that? Clare asked, not really wishing to know.

"It's an Ouija-board" Rachel said full of confidence. "Come on; let's check out the spooks eh?

"I must say it makes me feel very uncomfortable, dabbling in black magic", she shivered.

"Don't be silly, it's just a bit of fun"

Rachel placed the old brown stained board on the table, moved from side to side, and looked up and around the building, as if checking the presence of anything spooky. Her Nan had always said to make the Séance as entertaining as possible, as people believed what they wanted when in a darkened room.

"Achem" she cleared her throat.

"Now place two of your fingers, from both hands on the board, like this" she elucidated. Clare moved her hands to the board, "I feel silly" she moaned.

"Oh hush ya silly cow, just do it..." Rachel sounded annoyed, which made the hairs on Clare's arms and neck tingle.

Rachel smiled under her breath, remembering how terrified she was when her Nan had first used to board.

"Now..... Fingers still" she gently slapped Clare's hand and nearly burst into her characteristic laugh once more.

The leaky tap was still plopping in the distance, but the cars had stopped going by.

"Clare spoke through her tight lips "what's happening?

"Shhhhhhhhhsh"

Both girls sat with their fingers on the board.

Rachel put on her deepest voice, nearly chocking as her throat reverberated beyond its normal manor.

"Is there anyone there? Speak to us, we mean you no harm, speak to us now"

Silence.

Just a plop.

And silence.

Clare felt the board move, very slightly. Her breath began so shorten. The rusty dial, surrounded by letters also started to twitch.

Rachel repeated her request.

"Don't be afraid, talk to us, we are here to help you"

Her Nan had gone into much greater detail, saying religious quotes and Latin. Which terrified the gathered participants.

She watched in total ore as the dial started to move, on its own. She took a sneaky peek at Rachel, whose hands were firmly on the board. Could she be blowing it? Her mouth was shut.

The dial moved to the letter C. Then very slowly to the letter A. Then to the letter T. Then it spun three times around the board and stopped precisely on the letter S.

"Cats" shrieked Rachel in a high pitched voice. "Cats, are there any cats in the building?

Clare was too stunned to notice that Rachel was staring at her, but then looked up, terrified.

"Not that I know of" she said and looked back at the board. Her left leg had started to twitch.

It was on the move again.

"I think someone used to keep chickens in the sheds" she added sheepishly.

The dial started spinning, anti-clockwise. It stopped at the letter L.

Clare couldn't believe she was seeing this, and gulped. Rachel had to stop herself from smiling at her friend's petrified state of mind. But even she was shocked at how the board reacted.

A was the next letter, then an N. quickly followed by a C, an A an S… a T……… it then began to spin so fast it became a blur.

"Lancaster" Rachel squealed "it's saying Lancaster"

Clare was very frightened, her leg was shaking. Even Rachel hadn't experienced it doing this so quickly and began to feel fear rising in her stomach.

"Make it stop" said Clare in a whimper. "Make it stop please"

"I cant, I can't" said Rachel, who's once confident voice had become a whisper.

It felt like Clare's fingers were glued to the board, she tried to pull her hands away, as did Rachel.

The curtains at the front of the pub bellowed viciously, knocking some empty glasses from a table, they bounced on the carpet and laid still.

Then the board flew out from beneath their hands, across the room.

It was spinning sideways, moving from side to side, as if searching for something.

It crashed into the wall where the picture of Captain Lancaster once hung, and smashed into small fragments of old wood. The dial plunged to the floor, still attached to a small piece of wood. It came to rest on the carpet, the dial still spinning. Slowly, as the girls watched it moved slower and slower, almost in slow motion. Then it stopped.

"That was a set up you crazy bitch" said Clare, who was quite angry.

"No, no, I mean not at all, I'm as freaked as you" They both started to laugh.

"But that was so fucking weird, how'd ya do it, string? Magnets?

"No, nothing I swear on me Nan's life"

Clare got up, rubbed her left leg, which had stopped twitching..." well that was unreal, I mean totally unreal, don't tell anyone about this will ya, they will think we are mad... nutters.... Loonies even".

"As the girls giggled themselves silly, Clare's ears twitched; it was that sound again. Rachel downed her drink. Still giggling she spluttered as a small piece of ice lodged in her throat and vodka started dribbling from her nose.

'Just call me a lady won't ya?' she howled as she wiped her arm across her face. 'Ssshhh ... listen.'

The two pals strained their ears, mock concern etched on Rachel's face. There was total silence. Rachel jumped up so quick that Clare's heart almost stopped and she ran towards the front doors.

'Come on ya bastards,' she shouted up the stairs. There was nothing there. 'Must be them ghosts,' she said, laughing and started to flail her arms about and wooing loudly.

'Course, you know what they say.'

Clare felt another joke coming as Rachel slumped on the sofa, causing it to rise at one end.

'Why are demons so friendly to ghouls. Because demons are a ghoul's best friend. Get it? Diamonds etc.'

Clare groaned. 'Yeah, yeah, not one of your better ones,' she nodded, suddenly feeling very tired.

Rachel climbed into her old battered red mini, still laughing. 'Wooooooo ...ha ha ...wooooo,' looking up at Clare as she watched from the window. Then she noticed a man looking out of another window on the second floor. 'He's quite good looking in an old fashioned sort of way,' she thought. 'Got a uniform on as well, the kinky minx.' She was about to shout up at Clare 'You dirty litt...' but Clare's face was gone. So was the man's.

'She's got a fella in there, the filthy little cow. No wonder she wanted me to go so early.' She felt a pang of jealousy and envy. 'I bet he is an officer but not a gentleman.' Her imagination started to wander. 'The naughty minx,' she thought again and tutted loudly and laughed as her grumpy car engine rattled up the coach passage to the quiet High Street. She beeped her horn five times and shouted out the open window, 'whaahay.' Give It Away blaring from the CD player as she roared off down the street, tutting, 'the naughty little minx.'

Clare left the tills under the bar; near a piece of old sandstone. She remembered seeing it in the upstairs flat, holding the heavy wooden door to the stack room open, suddenly she felt really tired. She put the two empty glasses in the dishwasher and, wiping the bar one more time, walked towards the back doors.

Something made her turn around. Through a small gap in the curtains a sparse beam of lamp light cast almost a spotlight shape on the panelled walls, and the drawing of the Captain was back in its place. The glass reflected the light and as she looked around the building in every mirror she could see his eyes watching her. It was a cold steely stare, very intense and piecing, although he appeared to be smiling. The frame was gently moving from side to side with a soft bumping noise, almost a rhythmic pattern… almost like the distant sound of horses cantering. There was no sign of the board.

Her ears twitched again; she could hear the curtains flapping and walked a little faster, slamming the heavy doors. Feeling slightly nervous at spending the night in the stable flat on her own, but dismissing the cold lump of fear which hung in her belly, she was asleep three seconds after her head hit the pillows.

Deep in her sleep, at about 4.00am Clare's eyes suddenly opened. There was movement at the foot of her bed. Still half asleep she reached over to the bedside lamp and clicked it on. The light hurt her eyes, which she rubbed slowly: a long gapping yawn escaped her mouth.

On the bottom of the bed were two black and white cats, their bright eyes squinting in the harsh bulb light. They were purring intensely.

"Well hello there…. Awwwwww… come here" she beckoned the cats to come nearer.

The more confident one let out a loud meeeew and climbed up the duvet, sniffing its way up the bed. She reached out and cuddled it, it was so friendly.

"You're a lovely little chap aren't you" she beckoned the other over, and it almost leaped at her… The two cats started to play fight and roll around the bed. Both were purring their heads off.

Clare began to laugh, and the two cats were now playing chase the tail: jumping up on the pillows, running across the head board the disappearing under the duvet. Their two little heads making small bumps as they continued to romp.

"You're crazy" Clare squealed and crawled under the duvet to find them and give them a huge cuddle.

"Where did you go then? Eh…. I'm coming to get you" She made a slight growling sound which made her feel quite silly.

She pulled up the duvet. The cats were gone. She looked under the pillows, slipped off the bed to look under it. She got out of bed and walked around. All the windows were shut, so was the bedroom door.

The cats were gone.

"But" ……. Feeling puzzled, she pulled open the curtain, and looked out into the pub car park. It was pitch black. She opened the rusty window, which creaked loudly and peering on tip toe out into the black woods and could just vaguely hear purring. Then scuffling. Then silence.

She climbed back into bed, turned off the light and smiled. She could still feel at the foot of the bed two lumps, moving about. But resisted the temptation to investigate further, and drifted back into a deep dream filled sleep.

She didn't notice the half eaten rabbit, and a mouse with no head gently placed on one of the pillows.

The next morning was warm and very bright. She bounded up the metal back stairs at 8.56, keen to impress the manager of her competence and ability. He was back at lunchtime, so she busied herself in a cleaning frenzy, humming Give It Away, and occasionally dancing on one foot. An hour later, as the kettle popped, she took a well-earned break for a coffee and a smoke. Walking up to the main bar, she picked up the tills and noticed the stone had gone, and an empty glass. She sniffed it; it was fresh whisky. On a silver tray was an old bottle, and a cobweb had attached itself to the bar. The curtains at the front of the pub bellowed out, flapping around the windows and she heard a soft thud and a jingle of metal. Across the road, the bells rang. It was 10.00 am.

1916...

As the shell exploded six feet way, his whole body shook, sending him flying into the air. He landed in a crumpled heap and was winded, gasping like a fish in the desert. An eerie silence followed; then, as acrid smoke and shrieks of agony from his comrades rose in the dark night, his right arm and leg were numb. A hand perched from the soil; he recognised the ring on the finger; it was Smithy. He crawled on his good side and clasped it.

'Ok mate? You ok mate?' As he pulled, all that come from the dirt was the remains of an arm, still smouldering. Anger swelled in his heart.

'Jesus, how can this be happening?'

His mind went back to less than a week ago, in the pub, laughing, joking. The warmth of the people, the bargirl with green eyes. The pub cats wandering around the bar, revelling in affection.

He had had an excellent fish supper that night, with fresh new potatoes and peas from the garden, he remembered the texture of the white meat and the lemon cheesecake afterwards as he sat bloated but happy with a pint of ale and a woodbine in his hand: now he was in a foreign land, staring death in the face.

He looked up at the beaming half-moon, about to scream when a sniper's bullet smashed into the left side of his helmet, spinning him round into a ditch of cold muddy water.

None of his friends made it through the night as he lay in the dirt, slurping at the putrid water and blood that kept him alive. His left arm and leg had been toasted, but somehow the bullet had just passed his left ear. When he came to he was shaking so violently two soldiers held him to the cart rail. He screamed as his blackened skin came into contact with the rough surface.

'Easy there, Ronnie. Can't you see the lad's in pain? And getting that toxic shock syndrome no doubt an' all. Easy lad.'

The medic drew a syringe from a big bag, peaked it and plunged it into his good arm.

'That should help.'

A dose of pure morphine flooded into his blood, and, as he stopped shaking, Eddy looked at the men. Through a haze he saw faces; he saw the girl with the green eyes. As the drugs calmed him he was back in the public bar; he heard the music, the laughter. Smiling faces filled his mind. Just as he slipped

into a coma he was saying 'mama ... mama ... ma.' His fists were clenched tight like a baby's.

'He might just make it, this one, he's a fighter.'

They laid him down gently and covered part of his still face with a Hessian blanket. There were tears running down one side.

'Poor bastad, so young. Curse this fucking war.' The medic said and angrily threw the syringe to the floor. It shattered into a thousand pieces as he stared at the endless line of smashed men; some with mouths agape; some with no faces; most openly weeping.

The cottage hospital at East Grinstead was small and well organised. Private Edward Jones sat up for the first time unaided, wincing as his body felt like glass paper. Realising that every broken man in the tiny ward had lost friends and relatives, he muttered a quiet prayer to himself. No one spoke, the silence was calming. One nurse had dropped a tray on the floor and the noise was almost ear shattering. Several of the men lapsed into their nightmare state cowering under the sheets and wetting the bed. Matron telling them off like little children, although with a deep compassion and an aching heart.

After four weeks the pain and soreness of the burns had eased, the nightmares that made sleep impossible were fading. The same images all the men had, of their friends, twisted and blackened, arms outstretched as if seeking guidance from God. He was alive and home.

After two months the physical wounds had nearly healed and he had made some new and good friends, their grief bonding them as a shared nightmare. And one nurse, with her long flowing auburn hair neatly pinned under her hat, always smiled at him, making the boredom bearable. Her pretty eyes made his insides flutter.

His dear old mum brought grapes and apples, and tales from the town of new and exciting shops opening. She waffled on about her latest hat and the horse poo that littered the town. He listened, not wishing to be rude, but a cold lump formed in his stomach as the post arrived from the coast. He recognised the army envelope and opened it slowly, fear causing his belly to rumble.

'Ope they're feeding you good in 'ere. Going by the sound of that,' his mum said, 'you look a bit thin and' all. Need a good feed up when I get yous home. And that pretty nurse ... make a lovely wife she would.'

The nurse looked over and smiled.

'See, see, she likes you an' all. Last week the vic...'

He had been recalled to the western front.

'I said the vicar's wife was telling me of a smashin' wedden last week,' but he was not listening. The generals paid no attention to the daily carnage the men lived and breathed in. They were safe in big houses miles from the front lines, sipping French brandy and groping French whores, congratulating themselves on another three feet of land they had won.

He screwed the letter up and threw it on the floor.

'Mum, mum,' he shouted at her. 'I have to go back ... they want me to go back.'

She was still in mid-sentence.

'Go. Go where? I've got some nice cakes and some Indian tea, and the tree house your dad made is still in good order.

Could do with a lick of paint though, and ..'

'Shut up,' he screamed at her, ' just shut the fuck up.'

There was silence as he looked around the room. All the men's eyes were the same; they had all just read the same letter. Some started to weep; others hid under the sheets, wetting the bed.

'Well, if you're gonna take that tone with me, young man,' his mother began.

'Mrs Jones, please.' The nurse took her arm and led her away from the bed. 'He's just tired,' she explained. 'If you would like to come back tomorrow, I'm sure he will be better.'

His mum tottered off with the nurse.

'He is normally a nice polite young man, you know. Make someone a good husband one day. Did I tell you about my new hat? It's got ...'

The nurse smiled and waved her goodbye at the main doors.

'Thank you love. See you tomorrow then. Bring some grapes, I will, just for you... make someone a lovely wife you will.'

As the nurse returned to the ward, several of the men were being sick, some were shaking and some held their heads in their hands, weeping uncontrollably. Eddy was just staring into space. Somehow he knew he would never see his mum again; somehow the nurse knew she would never see him again.

He joined the new regiment and was set to embark the next day. His belly throbbed as he joined the new lads for a few drinks at the Dorset Arms public bar. A false sense of camaraderie echoed their drinking. Some of these lads were just seventeen and had never seen the trenches, smelt the smell of death, or felt the fear that it might just be your last night on earth.

He sipped his pint. 'You bloody poor bastards,' he muttered under his breath. Even at twenty-one he felt like a veteran because some of the lads looked about fifteen. Taffy Mcloud stood up on a table singing loudly in Welsh. His spotty chin and scruffy hair seemed out of place against the clean and starched uniform.

'Put a sock in it,' someone yelled, 'we ain't going on holiday ya silly bastad '

It was all too much for Eddy. He had been here before and seen similar men reduced to gibbering wrecks in hours. These new recruits had never seen, or smelled corpse filled trenches, Shattered lives or shell shock. Young men ripped apart whilst sharing a smoke. They were on a high from bravado; inside he was a broken man. He walked to the Saloon bar where at least there was some peace. The atmosphere was completely different; he looked around at the fine furnishing, the luxurious carpets and the elegant chandeliers that hung like great crystal palaces. There were huge slabs of ivory and gold marble, with the Earl's Of Dorset Crest positioned every few feet. Bell boys stood starched in certain corners, their fixed faces and eyes locked into the space in front of them, almost in their own world.

'You alright mate? Said Eddy to one, wondering if they were in fact status, the bell boy cast him a glance, and noticed his uniform.

He looked around, checking for any other staff, and nodded: 'yeah, doing good, got a light? I've got a box, but no matches'.

In one of his pockets Eddy had a spare box; he undid one of his many pockets and tossed them to the lad. Almost like lightening the lads arm shot out and caught the box.

'Cricket? Eddy said,

'Yup, I nearly got thrown outa school for whacking the ball so far it reached the boundary fence still about 20 feet in the air, crashed straight into the headmaster's greenhouse, knocked over about six pots and almost battered his sleeping cat' he laughed. He was about to continue the story but suddenly froze, his rigid face and body almost statue like.

Some guests moved silently into the saloon area, the ladies almost gliding in their fine dresses and regalia.

Eddy waited until they had passed, but noticed the sweet smell of summer jasmine, that hung in the air.

He nodded at the lad, who winked back: and continued his journey. Most of the furniture was antique, made of English oak or Yew, and the pastel colours and curtains combined with the smooth atmosphere made him feel very relaxed.

The carpets were so soft underfoot, most unlike the spit and sawdust environment of the public bar. He was glad he'd spent last night vigorously polishing his boots. It smelled of roses and Lilly of the valley, and in great ornate Chinese vases bizarre dried plants and seed pods poked upwards gracefully. Mouldings of French plaster cascaded their way around the ceilings, and on every lush wall, fine art and paintings framed in gold sealed cases sparkled in the light. He peered closer at one of the pictures; it was hand drawn in charcoal and was of an officer from the Crimean War. *Captain Jonathan Lancaster 1824-1855 RIP*. It was simply signed Simon De Montford.

'He must have seen a bit of action,' he said to the immaculately dressed young woman behind the bar. 'Look in those eyes; you can almost see the fear he was feeling.'

'That was drawn by one of the last managers here,' she said. 'Must have known him, I suppose. A few years ago, though. My father was telling me a story about that picture. Apparently, just two days after he put it there, he dropped dead in the cellar, had a heart attack. They found him in a corner. White as a sheet he was. They say it was because he had seen a ghost.'

'A ghost? Eddy mocked. He thought of all the death he had witnessed, and the thought of ghosts and lost souls made him feel edgy.

He mooched around the saloon, checking if the other pictures held similar stories. A Lord here, a Lady so-and-so there. A fat chief with a large carving knife grinning.

'Quite an historic place, this,' he said as he leant on the bar. 'Seen some people come and go. Makes you think, doesn't it? All we are, just leaves that fall, year after year.'

'Ok there, Captain Doom,' the woman said smiling, 'got the world on your shoulders have you?'

Her warmth made him lighten up.

'Just been recalled. Western Front, France. We leave in the morning.' His mouth went very dry. 'The Somme or some shitty hell hole.' He felt sick with anger. 'Some fucking shitty hell hole, filled with mud and shit and death and…' He broke down.

She came around to him, holding him tight. The bar was not busy; an elderly couple in the corner looked over down their noses and tutted.

'What you fucking looking at?' He screamed.

'Sshhh.' she stroked his hair. He was shaking with rage. The elderly couple rose to their feet and walked to the back doors.

'These youngsters today, no respect,' muttered the woman.

'Would have been horse-whipped in my day,' the old man stuttered. 'Discipline, there's just no discipline these days. I blame that Lloyd George fella.'

The back door slammed and Eddy, slowly becoming calmer, nearly jumped out of his skin. Even though she was only twenty-two she felt a mothering instinct towards the disturbed young man.

'Don't worry, she said softly, 'Ya daft bugger, dry your eyes. It will be al right.'

Feeling very foolish, he sniffed loudly.

'Yeah, you're right, I'm so sorry; it's just ..'

'Don't even go there.' Her voice was barely a whisper. 'Go back to your mates. The war will be over by Christmas, you wait and see. And when you come back I might even let you buy me a drink. How's that sound?' she said, blushing, realising the attraction was mutual.

He thanked her again, kissing her lightly on the cheek.

'I might just do that,' he said and, taking one last look at the charcoal drawing, he felt a surge of pride and pushed out his chest, straightened his back and moved silently to the public bar.

'Waahay.' The cheers and rowdiness as he walked into the smoke-filled room shook him.

'It's the uniform mate,' yelled Taffy. 'Them girls can't resist, you sly old dog, leaving ya mates to sneak off for a knee trembler with the bar girl.'

They couldn't have been more wrong as the dirty laughter echoed around the building, but he smiled when he thought of her green eyes, her soft warm body and the deep smell of her summer jasmine perfume.

Taffy had graduated to the bar now, clambering up, he said in a loud and dignified voice, 'My Lords and Ladies, gentlemen of the ... Where are we?'

'Dorset Arms,' someone muttered.

'Ahh, gentlemen of the boozer, drink my friends for tomorrow we head to the great shit hole in the sky.' He downed his pint.

Eddy noticed on Taffy's hand, a silver ring; it glowed like a gem, a soft and mesmerising silver light. For a second he thought of Smithy and remembered talking to him before the blast that tore him to pieces. The images started to flood his mind and he felt the icy cold lump almost burst inside his belly. He started to choke and began to weep. The other lads were still sinking their pints, unaware of his condition. He walked slowly out of the bar, looking for the kind woman who touched his soul. Frantically he paced up to the bar in the saloon area, but she was not there, another girl was working.

'Where is she ... the girl ... green eyes? Where is she? He said desperately.

'Oh, you mean Sarah. She left about five minutes ago.' The girl squinted her face. 'And good day to you as well, sir.

East Grinstead, "Dorset Arms" Hotel.

Tears were streaming down his face as he stumbled to the back doors. He heard them slam over and over and a loud whistling noise as the shells screamed in the night. He could not go back to that hell and see his new friends torn and ripped to shreds. The stairs that led to the cellar looked enticing and he raced down them, through several wonky corridors until he found a small room, full of old broken chairs and pieces of an old bath. On a corner table was an old chipped porcelain vase, and a strange looking piece of sandstone. He leant against the wall and got out a packet of cigarettes from his top pocket, dropping most of them on the floor because his hands were shaking so violently. He reached for his lighter, which he then also dropped onto the floor.

'For fucks sake,' as it hit the concrete and burst into flames. He stared at it mesmerised, as it danced like a yellow cobra. He stood up, but the rush of blood to his head sent him crashing into an old cupboard, which wobbled and fell almost in slow motion. It hit the floor and burst open and its contents spewed out. Some old newspapers and jars of nuts and screws littered the room.

Then he saw it. A tatty worn revolver sat there in front of him. He ducked as he heard another shell swishing over his head and grasped the gun. He put it to the left side of his temple and pulled the trigger. It clicked once; he saw Smithy's arm next to him. It clicked twice; he saw the men with no faces, crying for their mothers. It clicked a third time; he heard another shell burst which sent men into the air like ants. It clicked four times, he heard someone screaming and gurgling as they lay face down in the mud, drowning in their own blood. It clicked for a fifth time; he saw the girl with green eyes, her soft warm body and the sweet smell of summer jasmine. The bullet passed his left ear through his brain and thudded into the solid oak beam behind him. He fell to the floor; he could see her smile. A small pool of blood formed by his leg and, like a child, he poked his finger in it and started writing on the wall.

He died at 9.56 pm. Upstairs in all the noise and smoke, Taffy was mooning his arse out the window at upstanding but outraged citizens. In the saloon bar the picture of the Captain fell from the wall and smashed into tiny fragments, and the girl with the green eyes felt a shiver run right down her spine as she crossed the road by the pub.

Every one of the men in the new regiment was dead by the end of the week. Taffy had a nervous breakdown and was shot behind the railway station at Ypres for being a coward. In a letter sent home to his mother in Wales, the army solicitor said her son had fought bravely and she should be proud he had died for his country.

1994...

Pushing the long straggly hair away from his face, and sweating like a horse, the drummer dropped the last case, each weighing the same amount as a small elephant. Setting it up was easy, but at least now, in the cosy room at the back of the Dorset cellars, the kit could remain, except for gigs and recording. Just flick the switch, turn on the amps and PA, and bingo! A rehearsal room was born. His breath streamed out of his body and he was puzzled as to why the room got so cold. When he first came in it was warm and he was sweating.

The pub upstairs was always full of students and at week-ends bands played in the old restaurant on the first floor. The poor old place was being slowly battered alive by very loud music on all three floors. One exception was the other band he played in, called the Twelve Sullivans. What they lacked in volume was compensated by an adrenaline, energy and Guinness consumption of vast proportions. The building creaked and groaned as the lead singer, guitar in hand, climbed up onto the large PA system just so he could get the crowd to jump even higher. There were not twelve of them, neither were some of them Irish, but the atmosphere was electric and at the end of the evening hoards of revellers staggered down the stairs to the front doors, still singing 'All for me grog, 'A pub with no beer,' 'Danny Boy' and 'The wild rover' as they weaved, hugged, laughed and slurred their way home.

But the room in the cellar was cold, and the fuses and bulbs kept blowing. With the musical gear set up the band could wander in and rehearse together or on their own. Or just to meet up and discuss forthcoming gigs, and the girls that would be there, sweating and screaming.

'Tell you what,' said the drummer, 'I can't be in there on my own any more.'

There was an eerie silence.

'It's just that it feels like there is someone else in there with you.'

128

Howey, the bass man nervously spoke

'That frosted glass window. There is a face looking in some-times. I put a piece of paper on it, but it still felt weird. I ran out the door and shouted, but there was no-one there... nothing... Freaked me right out. When I went back inside the room was freezing.'

'One night last week,' spoke up the singer, 'I was go-ing through some harmonies, just singing to myself. When I stopped, the singing carried on. It sounded like a little girl. I grabbed the door, but it was stuck and the handles were ice-cold, my hand stuck to them. When I finally got out ... well, I'm sorry but I just can't go in there again. I spoke to the manager and he said that, for security the doors were all locked, you can get out easily enough, but no-one can get in.'

They decided not to rehearse that night, being as they had managed to freak each other out so much. A beer or two was called for. As the drummer walked up the stairs, Howey had a large songbook in his hand which, just before they got to the safety of the upstairs, he dropped with a loud crash. Drum-boy ran up the last five stairs as the other two fell about laughing.

'You bastards,' he said as his trembling hand clutched a pint of Guinness, spilling the first mouthful all over himself. One of the girls came over and wiped the bar.

'Wass up with you then? Just seen a ghost or something?'

A thin smile came over his face and his eyes wandered, looking in the direction of the cellar.

They had arranged with the manager to have the room checked out. Electricity was a dangerous thing and with just one loose connection, someone could be fried to a crisp.

'So that's why your hair stands on end, is it?' Howey said to the singer, 'you said it was hair gel.'

Three more pints arrived but the drummer was still nerv-ously tapping on the bar with his fingers. Within the hour an electrician had arrived and the drum-boy's belly gave off a low rumble as the five of them headed back to the cellar.

'You know the rules, mate. No farting in a confined space.'

They all laughed loudly, except the drummer, who peered over the banisters, sheepishly.

The room was exceptionally warm and drum-boy had pulled on his coat, even though it was sunny outside, and the jokes continued.

'But how come it's so warm in here?' said Howey. 'It's usually bloody freezing.'

The manager looked at them in disbelief.

'Well, you're right next to the boiler room. Theoretically you should be baked alive. You could fry an egg on the top of that thing.'

The sparky checked all the plugs on the equipment, then the wall sockets and finally the light switches, his little red box omitting bizarre noises and flashing intermittently.

'Everything appears to be okay, but I'm not a happy bunny.'

Someone in the room laughed.

'It doesn't make sense. There seems to be an external power source coming from ...' He turned around, looking puzzled. Drum-boy held his butt cheeks together and the giggles started. 'There.' He pointed to the wall.

'Yeah, right,' said the manager. 'So the wall is generating it then.'

Howey snorted and put his hand to his face, muffling his rising laughter.

'Well, not as such. What's behind it anyway?'

'The hanging gardens of Babylon, maybe?' Howey couldn't resist.

'Herds of wildebeest grazing on green meadows?' Even Drum-boy was starting to smile. 'A room full of naked women?'

'Now that would be nice,' said the sparky, grinning like a Cheshire cat.

The manager swung the small club hammer at the wall, expecting it to just bounce off, but instead, the hammer, his arm and half his body plunged into a large gap. 'What the f..!'

He pulled himself out, dusting bits of plaster off his head and spitting out small pieces of wood, laughing at his own dumbness. It was all too much for the lads and they all burst into howls of laughter.

'You look like a fucking snowman,' said the singer, 'Oi, frosty, what's behind the wall today then children?'

The manager kept spitting out dust and muttered, 'Bloody 'ell, I wasn't expecting that.' Intrigued he grabbed a torch from the sparky's bag and, lurched back into the hole, white powder still floating in the air.

'Christ almighty....' He shone the torch into the abyss. There was another room, about the same size. With wild eyes he began to tear the plaster from the walls.

'Steady there, mate,' the sparky said, but the manager was ripping large pieces of the wall down. It was only a coarse timber and plaster frame and the dust rose like a cloud, covering all the men in a light white powder. Their eyes and mouths watered giving them an eerie appearance.

'You look like a gho...'

'Yeah, yeah, so do you, but uglier.'

As the wall smashing frenzy stopped the whole area was still floating with dust and dirt. Drum-boy's hair was tangled with sweat and stood on end, bits flopping to one side.

'Now you just look like a right tit.'

'Yeah, well so do you, but at least tits have a purpose.'

The laughing began again and the men stood giggling as the fine white powder faded, brushing their clothes and wiping their eyes.

The lights started to flicker and the sparky's little red box began to flash and wail.

'That's all we need, a bloody power cut.'

The light bulbs sporadically went off, and, in the darkness, on one of the walls, rectangular shapes started to appear. The dust seemed to be filtering away through a small hole in the corner and, as the room cleared, on every wall there were newspapers. In the darkness the manager tripped over an old piece of sandstone, laying by the door. The light flicked on then off, then on again. The manager's eyes started to bulge, and they all peered closer at the mass of cuttings, scraps and booming headlines.

Battle of Jutland published 1918..... The battle of the Somme..... 219,000 prisoners taken alive..... Trench warfare kills 5,000,000 ..... mustard gas kills 10,000..... Ypres falls .....

'Jesus,' said all the men, almost at the same time. 'this is endless.' On every piece of wall and ceiling, the old yellow and flaky news screamed out. Drum-boy touched one of the pieces and it melted into dust, sending a shiver down his spine. The sparky was reading the articles on the ceiling;

9,500 killed at Ardent ..... The Hildenburg line falls ..... Haig blamed for deaths ..... Lloyd George gives speech of his life .....

'It is just unbelievable,' said Howey. No-one was laughing or smiling now. The stony and ashen-faced men read in silence, each in turn swallowing hard as the facts sank in.

Gas attack kills 7,500 ..... corpses left to rot in fields ... gypsies scavenge troops pockets .....
One headline made all their mouths drop open.
10,000,000 men killed or missing ..... the Monarchy says prayers at St Paul's.

One wall was just filled with the names of men. It seemed almost endless. Brothers, uncles, fathers, sons.

The lights flickering again broke the silence. The red box started to wail and, almost shaking his head, the sparky spoke.
'Ther... th...' He was so lost in the thought of it all he could barely speak. 'There must be a problem somewhere in this room.'
'You're fucking telling me,' said Howey, with not a trace of humour in his voice.

The electrician moved the box closer to one of the walls; it wailed a single mournful note.

'There is something behind here.' He scratched at the newspaper, which just fell off in dusty clumps. There was wallpaper underneath which came away just as easily, and the vague outline of a solid oak beam emerged. Running to one side was the original mains power cable, over one hundred years old, and lodged; half-embedded in it was a single bullet. It had just missed breaking the cable by millimetres. They all stared at it, mouths open. Around the base of the beam there were scratch marks, made by a human hand, and pieces of nail were scattered on the floor. Written on the wall in old dried blood were three words ... God help me. Outside they heard the church bell ringing. It was 10.00.

'I need a beer,' said Drum-boy.

'I need a gallon,' said the manager.

'I need to go for a crap,' said the sparky.

'I need to leave this room,' said Howey.

The singer just stood and stared at the wall. 'I need to know what the hell happened in this room.'

The men moved slowly up the stairs to the bar. No-one spoke and even Drum-boy dragged his feet.

As they walked into the main area, which was full of people drinking, laughing and singing, the bargirl opened her green eyes wide.

'Bloody hell,' she said, pointing. The whole bar turned and stared.

The men grinned sheepishly.

'The five of you look like flippen ghosts...'

2666...

The main front doors of the Dorset Arms were shut and boarded up for the last time. The windows were covered in a thick steel mesh, and painted black. Some one had jokingly painted a red cross on the white walls. Nobody laughed.

Civil war had been declared in England, as over the last 200 years tens of thousands of immigrants had pushed the country to breaking point, and most major cities were anarchic chaos.

In the 30 years following 1997, over two million people from across the world had descended upon this green and pleasant country. The powers that be oblivious the consequences.

Families fought for small patches of green land, whole communities spoke their own language, had their own laws and religious beliefs: any person who showed the slightest bit of resistance or belief in the old ways was crushed with brutal and savage violence. Central Government had relocated to Southern Europe, Existing in a massive steel and concrete labyrinth of caves and underground tunnels. Only surfacing to be flown by helicopter to exotic and private beaches in and around Australia and New Zealand.

For those who remained, too poor to flee, life was intolerable. It moved on... but the fear of violence and death at the hands of religious fanatics was a ghost that haunted everyones lives. The huge housing boom of early 2000 had covered most of southern England, towns and villages merged. Cities became overrun with disease and poverty. The mortality rate had slipped back to the figures of the early 13th century, as the human immune system went into meltdown. Fresh water was scarce, fresh food was unavailable, and most people took to growing their own fruit and vegetables, keeping a small array of animals and beehives and becoming self sufficient.

People were threatened or killed for a potato, or a cherry.

Everything that represented 'The old way' was banished. Churches were pulled to the ground, their bells silenced. Anything that was seen to be English, or patriotic was destroyed to beyond recognition. Alcohol was banned and women went back to being third class citizens, treated like animals and beaten on a regular basis. Total male-chauvinistic and ancient attitudes ruled with a fist of iron.

Global warming had flooded most of the low lying areas of the country: Essex did not exist anymore. Most of Norfolk was underwater, and the sea salt was slowly poisoning the land. For once such a green and pleasant Island, it was slowly becoming strangled to death by human excrement, rotting bodies floating in rivers, and a new and utterly deadly strain of the plague was festering in the hearts, minds and souls of the remaining indigenous population.

On one of the many big grand round oak tables inside the pub on the first floor a feast was being prepared. Beef roasted in the oven, and fresh vegetables were being steamed in the kitchens.

6 bottles of Lamberhurst wine, 3 red, 3 white sat opened and breathing on a deep burgundy table cloth. Chrystal wine glasses had been especially polished, the knives and forks sparkled to perfection and large church candles flickered in the darkness, casting shadows against the cobweb covered walls. The interior furnishings had long since rotted away and thick layers of mould had risen through out the whole building.

The guests arrived in good time, each knowing exactly were to sit. The head chair was an old gothic masterpiece, rescued from the church before it was pulled to the ground. All the seats and fine wood carvings had been burnt to ashes.

The preacher and his family victims of a suicide bomber.

The five diners took their places, and sat down at the table.

Anne Tree said grace: 'Bless ye Lord, for what we are about to receive may we be truly grateful … Amen.'

She was at the head of the table, Mary Sumner sat next to her on her right, John Lancaster sat to her left. Edward Jones and Wilfred Bumble completed the circle of good friends, and after all saying 'Amen' the feast began.

'I say' said John 'these vegetables are rather good, cooked to perfection… and the beef.' He put his fingers to his mouth 'just perfection, is Digger not here to join us?'

'Wilf spoke out 'he's off chasing those posh birds with his muscles and spadesmanship' he laughed.

They all chuckled.

'Some wine good sire, we found it in the cellar. Traditional English wine' said Anne and filled his glass. They all stopped

eating for a second and raised their glasses: Anne had let Mary have just one glass full, as it was a special occasion.

'To friends then, Friends for life' they all downed their glasses, Mary quickly developing hic-cups.

'I- hic- can't -hic- eat-hic-eat-hic-my-hic-dinner-hic-like this-hic' she wailed.

Anne reached down into her basket of hidden depths, and pulled out a small hessian bag containing freshly crushed peppermint leaves,

'Come here girl, take a deep breath of this' and Mary put her nose into the bag and inhaled deeply.

She pulled her nose out; with bits of leaves stuck to her nostrils...the gang all stared and waited patiently...

'Yep, gone...' and she burst into laughter. The whole table roared with her.

Wilf spoke up again, with bits of beef fat wobbling around the corners of his mouth.

'Bleeden wonderful Anne, how do ya do it? Your one special lady, hey, a toast to Anne everyone' and he lifted his glass.

'Hear hear' and their glasses clinked together.

'I think a toast to Mary for such a spread is in order,' and again the glasses clinked. Mary blushed but held her head up with pride. This was her family, this was her home.

'I think a toast to Farmer Wilmington for this succulent piece of beef is also in order' said John.

'Hear hear' Said Anne.

They filled their plates again.

Mary had had three glasses and was becoming quite tiddely, 'Lady Sackville shed' she slurred 'Shees bringing me some right posh china marbles from her eastern travels,' then she stood up proudly, wobbled and declared:

'A toast to my mate, and I'll wooop the lot of your lardy backsides any day... hic, I'm the marble champ me.'

They all smiled; and felt an overwhelming warmth for this feisty and beautiful young woman.

'I think you should be sticking to water from now on young lady' scolded Anne softly and as Mary sat down she belched, 'Pardon me for being so rude, it was not me it was my food' she cackled and the table erupted into laughter again.

'Hey Johnny boy' said Wilf, found me some top notch whiskey in the cellar' and he pulled out from his tatty coat a bottle of fine single malt, which made John's eyebrows raise in appreciation.

'Hummm, very nice.'

'A little after dinner tipple would certainly fit the occasion, what do you say my good fellow?'

'A delightful idea good sire,' John replied. 'I'm a bit partial to a drop of the good stuff.'

After dinner the friends retired around the fireplace, Anne gently poked the roaring flames with an iron rod, making sure the heat built up nicely, filling the cold and empty pub with warmth. No-one outside could see the smoke from the chimneys; they were too busy hiding behind closed doors.

Wilf stumbled off for a piss, a drunken smile on his happy face, and he began to sing 'Gotta keep moving on' occasionally dancing on one foot.

'Don't get lost Wilfy' shouted Anne

'Take the left hand corridor, and don't forget to put the bloody bog seat down after you peasant'

'Yes Mama' he said and stumbled down the right hand corridor.

Mary had eaten so much she pulled up her crisp white shirt to reveal her big bloated stomach,

'Well look at me belly, looks like im bleeden pregnant' she screeched.

John had finished the bottle of whiskey, and asked Anne to dance. They did a slow waltz around the first floor, with Mary, Wilf and Eddy singing 'La la laa la, la la laaaa la' and pretending to play violins.

His boots giving off a slight jingle of metal at every graceful step.

Eddy felt really happy; he was home at last, with his friends.

No more trenches, no more death. Just soft warm peace.

As they all sat down again around the roaring fire, Anne brought out a pouch of her home made smoke, and packed one of Digger's long clay pipes to the brim with the aromatic hemp.

Mary took two puffs and collapsed in a coughing fit...

'Euuurrgh, how can you people smoke that shit?' and downed half a cup of water almost in one. The hic-cups returned.

Anne passed the pipe to Wilf who took a long deep lungful, and blew the smoke out from his nose, which made Mary giggle. He then sat back in a cloud of smoke with a big grin covering the whole of his face.

Eddy had found in a cupboard by the stack room a large piece of sandstone, shaped like a head and began to carve the face of a beautiful young woman, using Mary as inspiration. She tried to sit still, wriggling about and fidgeting: in her hand she clutched her best purple marble, squeezing it gently.

'Oh for God's sake woman, sit still' Eddy said smiling,

'Can't' Mary replied and pulled a face like a bloated pig.

'If the wind changes direction your face will stay like that' Anne warned,

Mary relaxed her body and face, but still had her green eyes crossed and stuck her tongue out defiantly.

She soon relaxed enough for Eddy's skilled hands to work on the stone because the two black and white cats had just wandered in the room, and were sitting by her feet...Purring their heads off as she very gently stroked them both.

Time stood still.

It was 10.00.

Anne Tree.

Wilfred Bumble.

Captain Johnathan Lancaster.

Miss Mary Sumner.

Private Edward Jones.

The Cats.

Credits...

I would like to thank the following people:

The East Grinstead Town Museum for the post card pictures.

http://www.eastgrinsteadmuseum.org.uk/

Jason and Wendy Hodge.

Pat Edwards.

The Aussie girls, Cardy Brodrick, Jay Deeie, Candice Humphreys, Laura Williams and Hollie Robb: Who always filled the Dorset Arms with fun, energy and mischief...!

Philip Hall and Hilary Gibbs at Ideas2Print ltd.

About the Author

Bonx Trigwell was born and grew up in the Crystal Palace Area of South London, England.

He moved with his parents to East Grinstead, and as a teenager explored the Dorset Arms, then still a hotel in great detail: as one of his new friend's Parents were the managers.

He studied Classical, Acoustic and Electric guitar, and has performed all over the UK with bands: Anerly Park, (Jazz Fusion) Karma, (Jazz Rock) The Bullfrogs (Blues) and his own band Pump (Funky Rock)

He won a silver cup at the Southampton Jazz festival and went on to be a guitar session player in London, and has been interviewed on BBC radio many times. He has also appeared on Mercury FM, Meridian FM, about his music and writing.

He also has a great passion for working in Sussex country house gardens, and recently completed designing a five acre plot overlooking part of the Sussex Weald.

And finds the history and architecture of East Grinstead's Medieval High Street and the people who have lived and worked in the Historic market town a compelling fascination.

At present he Lives in East Grinstead, with 9 guitars and 24 house plants.